"Hey, Sierra."

He had the same movie-star smile. Same devil-may-care stance. Same cheeky grin that could smooth out even the most ruffled of feathers. His voice, though, was deeper and silkier, like fine bourbon aged extra, and that sexy tone rolled her name into three distinctive syllables: Cee-Err-Uh.

In person he was far more handsome than the picture in last week's *New Charles Gazette*. She'd doodled devil horns onto his head while eating a breakfast of brown sugar cinnamon oatmeal. Then she'd recycled the newspaper and wondered what her therapist might say about the torch she both carried for him and wanted to burn him with, depending on the day.

"Jack," she acknowledged, making sure she used his given name and not the second nature "jerk."

"How are you?" he called, his pleasant tone holding just the right hint of masculine huskiness to spike her adrenaline in a way that proved sixteen years apart hadn't been enough.

"Fine," she replied, trying to play it cool. Especially if by *fine*, one meant freaked out, insecure, nervous and emotional, or the same way she'd always felt around him, back when her insides turned into marshmallow goo whenever he spoke her name. But this wasn't high school.

Dear Reader,

Until several years ago, I lived in a historic river town, one smaller than the fictional world I created in this story but no less beautiful. For eighteen years, I drove winding bluff roads that offered sweeping views of farms, vineyards and the Missouri River bottom, all of which became inspiration for Sierra and Jack's story, my twenty-fifth title for Harlequin.

I've always loved enemies-to-lovers stories. There's nothing quite like second chances and a righting of wrongs. Sierra James hates Jerk (real name Jack) Clayton for an act of high school cruelty. No way will she let him buy her family's vineyard. She may have left her naval officer career behind, but she's still a seasoned warrior. Sure, she might have written in her kindergarten diary how she wanted to marry Jack, but now he's enemy number one. For Sierra and Jack, finding their way back to the nirvana of one long-ago kiss will be a battle of the heart and soul. Toss in cookie dough and some vino, and All's Fair in Love and Wine.

I hope you enjoy this second book in the Love in the Valley series. Feel free to sign up for my newsletter at micheledunaway.com and send me email through my website. I love hearing from readers.

Cheers,

Michele

All's Fair in
Love and Wine

MICHELE DUNAWAY

HARLEQUIN
SPECIAL
EDITION

Recycling programs
for this product may
not exist in your area.

ISBN-13: 978-1-335-72459-5

All's Fair in Love and Wine

Harlequin Enterprises ULC
22 Adelaide St. West, 41st Floor
Toronto, Ontario M5H 4E3, Canada
www.Harlequin.com

Printed in U.S.A.

In first grade, **Michele Dunaway** knew she wanted to be a teacher when she grew up. By second grade, she wanted to be an author. By third grade, she decided to be both. Born and raised in Missouri, Michele lives in her childhood hometown and travels frequently, with the places she visits inspiring her writing. A teacher by day and novelist by night, Michele describes herself as a woman who does too much but doesn't know how to stop, especially when it comes to baking brownies and chocolate chip cookies.

Books by Michele Dunaway

Harlequin Special Edition

Love in the Valley

What Happens in the Air

Visit the Author Profile page
at Harlequin.com for more titles.

A long time ago, a starry-eyed girl holding a Harlequin novel dreamed of writing one and seeing her name on the cover. This marks the twenty-fifth time she's done that. This milestone is dedicated to all those who made my dream come true, especially my readers, my editors, my family and my friends; and to my students who make me a better person: build foundations under your dreams and march confidently toward them.

"Where there is no wine, there is no love."
                                                          —*Euripides*

Chapter One

Cake flour. Brown sugar. Softened butter. Chocolate chips. A top-secret family recipe known to a rare few trustworthy souls. Funny how, even after years of flying fighter jets, the step-by-step directions remained as routine as a preflight checklist. Taking comfort in the task's familiarity, Sierra James opened the commercial refrigerator and removed a metal sheet covered with a dozen chocolate chip cookies, all formed with slightly hollowed out centers. Into each depression she dropped a #40 scoop full of chilled batter, until all twelve cookies mimicked the shape of tiny sombreros created from delicious dough.

She put the current batch into oven three. After she set the timer for ten minutes, the oven to her left chimed. When she pulled on the handle, oven two blasted out 375-degree heat and sent an aroma of melted chocolate wafting to her nose. She removed the cookie sheet. Once she set that on a rack to cool, she started the entire process over, using the same steps her grandmother had taught her daughter, Sierra's mom—who'd showed them to Sierra and her younger sister, Zoe. It had been Zoe's dream to follow in her mom's footsteps and be next generation to own the store, and Sierra was glad of it. She'd help out, like she was doing today, but that was enough for her. She'd followed her dad and gone into the Navy.

Tradition meant quality, even if baking this way was slow and cumbersome. Six wall ovens ran simultaneously, baking the two-inch-high chocolate chip cookies that had made Auntie Jayne's Cookies world famous. Some in town would say the store had helped to put Beaumont's historic Main Street on the map. Sierra agreed cookies were a tastier draw than the riverside town that had hosted Lewis and Clark's expedition, or the Woman in White, the town's resident ghost and current star of this month's Halloween ghost tours. She'd been sighted for hundreds of years wandering along several blocks of Main Street, including this one. However, Sierra had never seen the famous spirit, nor had her sister, Zoe.

Sierra didn't necessarily believe in ghosts, even if she had seen some strange things while flying.

But it was cookies that commanded her attention today, not unexplainable atmospheric disturbances. Since she'd had a free Saturday afternoon—when lately did she not?—she scooped more dough, satisfied she'd prepared it correctly.

Like life, baking could be unpredictable and temperamental. The dough might not rise correctly for any number of reasons, including Missouri's fluctuating humidity or a slight temperature differential inside the oven. One or two degrees this way or that could ruin an entire batch. But Sierra enjoyed the challenge of beating the odds. Besides, there was something about creating the cookies the old-fashioned way, or crafting them with love as her mom said. It soothed a weary soul, and Sierra's could use all the help it could get.

Sierra stirred M&M candies into sugar cookie dough, moving the lever of the commercial stand mixer to speed four. The dough spun, thumped into submission and decadent deliciousness. No wonder her mom called baking therapy. The routine kept Sierra calm and stopped her from climbing the walls as she figured out her next steps. And there was the benefit of a tangible and tasty result.

At age thirty, she hadn't thought her career choices included baking cookies in her childhood hometown or working at her family's winery, but here she was. After the crash that ended her career, she'd had nowhere else to go, proverbial tail between her legs.

As a child, she'd loved living here and listening to her dad's tales of flying fighter jets over the ocean. Beaumont, though, was located in the center of the Midwest, hundreds of miles from the closest ocean shore. The Gulf of Mexico was twelve hours south down Interstate 55 or ninety minutes flight time. Sierra's zodiac sign—and her soul—demanded she be by water, and the older she grew, the more the Missouri River, rolling along two short blocks to the east of the store, failed to feed Sierra's soul. For her, the Emerald Coast had been paradise.

On a clear day, she'd fly her jet toward where water met sky, the greens and blues merging along the horizon, at that point where the only way to know which way was right side up was via instrumentation. Flying meant freedom and infinity. That moment, where one element started and the other began, that was when a navy pilot was master of her instruments and destiny. That life had been glorious.

Using more force than necessary, Sierra shoved the mixer lever into the off position. Those heady, deliberate days were done. They'd crashed and burned in a brilliant, blazing fireball that had lit up the Alabama night sky and brought bright orange daylight to a farmer's blackened field.

She lifted the bowl containing the cookie dough

and held it tightly to her apron-covered chest, the pressure stopping her body's desire to sit down. Inhaling deeply, Sierra concentrated on the task in front of her: grab a fresh scoop. Dip it into the bowl, then drop the cookie dough onto parchment paper. *Repeat. Repeat. Repeat.*

Calmer, Sierra put the M&M's candy cookies into an oven, set the timer and began laying out another sheet of parchment paper. Like a phoenix, she'd rise from the literal ashes. Returning to her childhood hometown had seemed a logical choice. Thankfully the well-meaning townsfolk, who knew her dream had died in the wreckage, had stopped giving her sympathetic smiles.

"Hey, Sierra!" Zoe hollered from the front room where she served customers. "We need more sprinkles and chips."

"Be right out." Sierra glanced at the digital display ticking down—she had plenty of time to refill the display cases before the cookies needed removing. She swapped out her plastic food-service gloves for a fresh pair. She opened the airtight storage container and removed a previously prepped display tray. Sugar cookies with sprinkles were a perennial favorite of younger kids, like Sierra's seven-year-old niece, Megan, and Megan's best friend, Anna Thornburg. In high school, Sierra had been a year behind Anna's dad, Luke. Luke had married his former high school sweetheart, Shelby, a few weeks ago. Shelby and Sierra had taken flying lessons together before the global adventure photographer had moved to Seattle for college. Now she was back permanently, and the town was delighted the two lovebirds had finally reunited after twelve years apart.

The only thing Sierra wanted to be reunited with was her plane.

But instead of doing loops in her navy-issued T-6B, she shuttled between her mom's cookie store and her dad's vineyard. The words *honorable discharge* tormented her—the papers finalized three months ago, a full year after the accident that clipped her wings. Navy Lieutenant Sierra James was no longer a flight instructor, but rather a civilian with PTSD that often kept her awake at night. When Luke and Shelby climbed into a hot-air balloon during Beaumont's annual balloon race the last weekend in September, Sierra had suffered a panic attack and needed to leave. The incident, only a few weeks old, remained another ugly reminder of Sierra's failings.

"Sierra!" Zoe yelled, her urging more insistent.

"Coming!" Irritated by how much her reflexes had dulled since arriving home, Sierra double-fisted two trays through the swinging door and into the front room. About eight people queued in a loose line, waiting for their turn to reach the counter. Two groups, Sierra assessed. Three minutes wait for each, at most. Her sister moved aside and Sierra traded the empty tray of chocolate chip cookies for a fresh, full one. She was in the process of swapping out the sprinkle cookies located on the bottom shelf of the glass display case when she heard a deep, masculine voice calling her name.

"Sierra? Is that you?"

Sierra lifted her hairnet-covered head and peered over the upper shelf. Only years of military training kept her eyes from widening in shock.

Jerk Clayton was standing in her store.

Like, the very same jerk who'd pulled her pigtails when she'd been in kindergarten and he'd been in second grade; and the very one who'd not given her the time of day in middle school unless he needed help with algebra, a class she'd taken two years early; and the very one who, her freshman year, had asked her to the homecoming dance—but only because of a bet from his asshole friends.

Luckily, her friend Emily had discovered Jack's real motives and told Sierra before she'd become the laughingstock of Beaumont High. Thankfully, he'd moved to Oregon two months later. One nemesis far removed.

Until here he was, like a bad penny turned up. Sierra closed the case's sliding glass door and straightened, wishing she were in her intimidating navy uniform instead of an apron and hairnet.

"Hey, Sierra." He had the same movie star smile. Same devil-may-care stance. Same cheeky grin that could smooth out even the most ruffled of feathers. His voice, though, was deeper and smoother, like fine bourbon aged extra, and that sexy tone rolled her name into three distinctive syllables: Cee-Err-Uh.

In person he was far more handsome than the picture in last week's *Beaumont Gazette*. She'd doodled devil horns onto his head while eating a breakfast of brown sugar cinnamon oatmeal. Then she'd recycled the newspaper and wondered what her therapist might say about the torch she both carried for him and wanted to burn him with, depending on the day.

"Jack," she acknowledged, making sure she used his given name and not the second-nature "jerk." She lifted the empty trays and stepped out of the way so Zoe could fill a customer's order box. Sierra edged toward the kitchen door, eager to escape.

"How are you?" he called, his pleasant tone holding just the right hint of masculine huskiness to spike her adrenaline in a way that proved sixteen years apart hadn't been enough.

"Fine," she replied, trying to play it cool. Especially if by fine, one meant freaked out, insecure, nervous and emotional, or the same way she'd always felt around him, back when her insides turned into marshmallow goo whenever he spoke her name. But this wasn't high school. She was a trained fighter who could shoot down an enemy without batting an eye. Running into Jerk Clayton should not make her pulse quicken, even if time had been exceptionally kind. Hell, the years he'd used growing into his skin had clearly been positively decadent.

She couldn't help but drink him in. Shiny dark leather Italian loafers stood in direct contrast to the checkerboard linoleum. The rolled sleeves of a burgundy shirt exposed all but a few inches of forearm under his elbow, revealing skin dusted with fine hair lightened by the sun. The crown on the gold watch circling his left wrist indicated the timepiece cost more than her car. The paper indicated he was an executive of some sort in his parents' company. Basically, the Claytons had more money than God, or at least far more than most of the residents of Beaumont.

"It's good to see you." He directed another friendly, easy smile her way and a tiny tremble filled her tummy, as if the first pangs of hunger surfaced.

Sierra fought against preening. She'd seen him work his charms on teachers and classmates alike. Need an extension on homework? Done. At one point that charm worked its magic on her, at least before she'd wised up. No reason for her heart to be fluttering as if the heater had kicked on. Her reaction must be the adrenaline of seeing a childhood nemesis, although, if she was honest, this adrenaline was different from the kind she experienced when flying near the speed of sound.

He stepped closer to the display case, careful not to get in the way of the kids choosing cookies. A dimple deepened. "You look great."

No man had a right to look as good as he did. Life on the West Coast agreed with him. Lighter highlights traveled through brown hair worn wavy and brushed away from his forehead, sort of like a younger Matthew McConaughey. Or a less coiffed Harry Styles, who was closer to Sierra's age of thirty. Jack's build, though, was all Chris Evans's Captain America. Her toes tingled as his greenish-blue gaze caught hers.

Sierra lifted an eyebrow she'd thankfully plucked that morning. "Still the flatterer, I see."

She gestured to the hairnet containing her pixie cut. Flour covered her black apron, and colorful sprinkle residue stuck to the long sleeves of her white shirt. "Then again, this fancy uniform is the height of Beaumont fashion."

Thick eyebrows knitting together told her she'd thrown him, but he recovered instantly. "Definitely trendsetting. Anything you wore always looked great on you. Still does."

"Still a player as well," Sierra quipped, refusing to squirm. She'd faced officers who'd made her quake in her boots; she could face a sexy, all-grown-up Jerk Clayton. Back in high school, had he meant what he'd said, she would have given him anything. Today she wouldn't give him an inch. Not after what he'd done. He was also proof that life truly wasn't fair. Why couldn't he be balding? Fat? Hunched over? Something?

She allowed a small, disarming smile. When facing the enemy, show no weakness. Give no parlay. Kill them with kindness, especially in front of tourists who would report seeing any drama or her caustic answers in their online reviews. "Are you back for a visit?"

Please say no.

The bells above the blue front door jangled as the first group of customers left. The second group moved forward, and Jack stepped farther in her direction. The counter forming a natural barrier, he lifted one of the slick Beaumont Main Street brochures from the clear acrylic holder. He flipped it open and gave it a quick once-over. "I arrived yesterday for a closing. I bought Sunny Days."

Sunny Days was one of the region's larger family-owned wineries. Sierra's family's vineyard considered Sunny Days its equal, not that Jamestown Vineyards worried much about competition. Her family's vineyard simply did everything better and produced a better product than anything in Beaumont County. "I didn't know that place was for sale."

Maybe she should have read that newspaper article instead of blackening his teeth.

Broad shoulders lifted in a subtle shrug as he

shifted his weight. "Everything's for sale if the price is right. I, well, my company, also bought Elephant Rock Vineyards and Primrose Hill. Got those places for a bargain."

"A Midwest bargain?" she clarified. Something she'd learned by moving first to the East Coast for the Academy and then to Florida was only Midwesterners revealed the price they paid. For instance, when one complimented a Midwesterner on their outfit, they'd promptly say where they got it, how much they paid and how much of a great deal it was. Same for their house, their car or their boat. Sierra had learned that everyone else found such revelations tacky. She tilted her head. "Must be nice to be back in the Midwest where things are bargain dollar."

"All sides were happy with the deal." He folded his arms across a broad chest, stretching the fabric.

Sierra averted her gaze and wondered if her parents knew this. Then again, they'd had a lot on their minds lately, even more after her arrival home. "You must really like wine."

"Something like that." With an evasive flicker of long eyelashes, he watched as her sister handed over a credit card receipt and a box of cookies. The minute the group left, he pivoted toward her. "Hey, Zoe. You're looking as great as these cookies. One dozen chocolate chip."

Sierra swore her sister actually blushed. Refusing to leave Zoe alone with the guy who'd always had a secret agenda, Sierra stayed put. She tried not to give in to temptation and bang the empty display trays together, as scaring off wild animals. Instead she watched as Zoe worked efficiently, her sole focus packaging cookies. Like Sierra, she was in uniform, but she wore a ruffled white apron that covered a prairie-style gingham dress. A grandmotherly white cap sat on her head.

"So, Sierra." Jack turned his attention back to her and spoke her name, this time as if tasting it. "Be for real this time. How's life been the past decade and a half?"

"Not as interesting as yours." She certainly didn't go around buying wineries on a daily basis.

He winked. "It's good for things to be interesting, wouldn't you say?"

Was he actually flirting with her? With Jack, she never knew. How many times had she misread him?

"Life would be boring if they weren't," Sierra volleyed easily, despite the lowered timber of his voice having turned her stomach into a dumb cliché of butterflies taking flight. She should be hitting him with all the zingers in her arsenal, tossing out grenades to incinerate the idea he could forget the past like yesterday's news.

Jack studied Sierra more intensely than a navy superior scrutinizing her military uniform. "So you work here."

"Sometimes. When the moon's full and if it's safe out."

He ignored her smirk. "I didn't know you lived here, that you came back."

"She's been in Florida," Zoe answered, indicating she'd been listening. Zoe moved the last of the cookies from the display tray to a square white box.

The jangling bell announced more customers, proof that Main Street remained a heavily trafficked tourist destination. While Zoe taped the lid, Jack tapped his credit card against the payment device, and his shirtsleeve inched up to reveal even more skin.

"So, Zoe. How's Ted?"

"We're divorced. Two years now."

For a brief moment mortification tinged Jack's lips, but then he laughed and made light. "I stuck my foot right into that one, didn't I? Sorry if I dredged up bad memories. He always was a fool, and still must be to have ever let you go."

This time Zoe did blush. Sierra bristled. A heartthrob never changed his wicked ways, and Jack the jerk had left devastated women behind him for miles. Including her. No way would she let that happen to Zoe.

"Since you closed your deal, I assume you'll be headed back to Portland?" Sierra asked, redirecting his attention before he asked about her two older brothers and dragged out this misfit reunion.

His left eyebrow lifted before the killer smile she swore he must practice in front of a mirror spread across his face. "Actually, no. Like you, I'm moving back. Could be for six months. Until the work's done."

Curiosity defeated her desire to shorten the conversation and shoo him along. "What work? Like renovations? Elephant Rock is a little worn down. But the vines are good and people visit."

The smile didn't slip, but it did soften. "My viticulturist and my vintner both agree on your assessment of the vines. It's far more than renovations. I have big plans."

"Beaumont never really changes."

That fact was one of the things that comforted her most. Outside, cars traveled over the centuries-old cobblestones unearthed by the town's council twenty-three years ago. Sierra loved the bricks, which showed that some things, like the historic buildings surrounding the quaint street, survived the test of time. Weathering only added character.

He lifted the box. "Everything changes. That's half the fun, wouldn't you say?"

Like a rough landing, his words jolted. In Sierra's case, change had been anything but fun. But bells jangled as more Saturday shoppers entered, this time a group of excited kids followed by their harried mothers. Time to usher Jack out the door. But before Sierra could speak, a striking platinum blonde with a skeptical expression creasing her brow stepped inside the doorway. She wore a stylish sundress and carried a designer purse that Sierra immediately envied. The woman lowered oversize square sunglasses and peered over the top. "Jack, are you about done? I didn't know buying cookies took so long. It's not like the place is that big."

Sierra let loose a pfft of breath. Of course she was with him. He was so true to type.

Facing the woman, Jack held up the square box. "Yeah, I'm done. Got a box of the best cookies anywhere. You'll find out when you try one."

"If you say so." The blonde's red-stained lip curled dubiously downward, making Sierra doubt the woman ate sweets. Too many carbs and calories. Sierra disliked her on sight and refused to let the blonde's derision stand.

"The proof's on the wall." Sierra pointed one of the trays toward the line of framed awards hanging on the far wall. She received a small sniff in response. Sierra puckered her lips to indicate her displeasure. Jack deserved her. Minus her outfit she had no taste, especially if she was with him.

The corners of Jack's lips rose. He'd seen Sierra roll her eyes after the woman's sniff. "What?" Sierra snapped, her tolerance for Jack's presence exceeded.

"Nothing." Jack's gaze lingered, assessing Sierra. She refused to squirm. "It was good to see you," Jack said, that deep warm honey tone with a slight husk adding, "I'm sure we'll run into each other again."

"Sure." A safe, throwaway word, meant to end the awkward conversation. Her running into Jack, even if he was back in town, was as probable as pigs flying. Or Sierra flying. Her gaze lingered as he exited the shop, his fingers pressing lightly on the blonde's waist as he guided her out the door. Then Sierra cursed as a faint rancid smell hit her nose. "Shit."

"Sierra! Not in front of the customers!" Zoe's admonishment landed on Sierra's backside, as she raced into the kitchen where the digital timer blinked the dreaded word: End. Sierra dropped the empty display trays into a deep stainless steel sink and the clatter joined the timer's frantic beeping. "Shit, shit, shit." Sierra grabbed the pot holders and withdrew the cookie sheets. While not charcoal—yet—inedible cookies did not meet the store's standard. Once again she'd let Jerk Clayton distract her, and because of him, she'd ruined the batch. Damn the man.

Damn her for still experiencing butterflies the moment he came into a room.

Sierra fought tears as everything from the past fifteen months slammed into her like a bullet in the back. The navy therapist had told Sierra her emotions might overwhelm at random times but Sierra refused to let that be an excuse. In an effort to check the flow of tears, Sierra sunk her top teeth into her lip, creating sharp pain. She was stronger than this. Better than this. By God, she would not devolve into out-of-control sobs.

With the baking sheets held low over the waste can, parchment paper and overbaked cookies slid off. They rustled and clunked into the trash can. She stared at the inglorious heap of crispy edges and acrid odor. She inhaled a steadying breath. They were only cookies. Not jet planes. Not her navy career.

The story of her life might be one of crash and burn, but all she could do was try again. Her parents had other, bigger things to worry about than Sierra's mental health. She was thirty, and she would get through this identity crisis. In order to have stability and familiarity, she'd already moved in with Mom and Dad—she would not burden them further by failing again.

Swapping out pot holders for a new pair of sanitary gloves, she reminded herself to take things one step at a time. Jack was a momentary distraction. A blip in her recovery and master plan. She would not let him sidetrack her. There were strides to make and cookies to bake.

Chapter Two

Carrying the box holding a dozen chocolate chip cookies, Jack Clayton guided Taylor from Auntie Jayne's. Perhaps his assistant's arrival had been fortuitous. Today was one of those weather-perfect days, and after a successful closing earlier, the last thing Jack wanted to do was get into anything with Sierra James, the one woman he'd never been able to figure out. Or forget.

He'd moved away from Beaumont High his junior year, and already most of the memories of his time there had blurred. But not those regarding Sierra. He remembered the day she'd rejected his offer to take her to homecoming and the subsequent fallout as if it had happened yesterday.

Despite this, when his parents declared they wanted to make Beaumont a seasonal home base, he'd understood. His parents had grown up here and been high school sweethearts. For them, the town was all rainbows and sunshine, and now, investment opportunity. Why not? Beaumont had a historic "it" factor, especially the historic downtown riverfront area that dated back to the late 1700s.

A pleasant October afternoon meant diners filled the outdoor cafés lining Main Street. Groups of tourists went from store to store, shopping bags in hand. Beaumont had been first settled by French explorers. Located between the Missouri River and the rolling hills that reminded early nineteenth-century Germans of their beloved Rhine Valley, the German settlers who arrived next had started planting grapes. Because of their efforts, the state of Missouri before Prohibition had produced almost as much wine as California. Now Missouri's wine industry consisted of approximately 125 mom-and-pop wineries. Outside of the streets of Historic Beaumont, a half-dozen of these places nestled into the countryside, existing as afternoon jaunts for the locals and those on day trips from St. Louis.

Jack and his family planned to change all that, bringing in guests from all over the country. Missouri sat in the middle of the country, and Beaumont was one hour or so outside St. Louis, making the town a perfect, central location to entice travelers. Transformation of Beaumont into a nationwide destination like the Napa, Sonoma or Willamette Valleys required vision and money. He had both.

The top down on his sleek silver Mercedes, Jack set the cookies on the back seat. He opened the driver's door and slid in, Taylor already in the passenger seat with her seat belt on. The car vibrated over the exposed cobblestones, and Taylor grimaced and shifted. "You'd think they'd pave these."

"Part of the quaint charm." This answer elicited a slight humph from Taylor. Turning left, Jack drove up a cross street—this one made of concrete. He headed out of town, the car's turbo boost tackling the winding, twisting Highway 49. The locals called this stretch "Winery Road" since there were six wineries within fifteen miles. After one of his parents' monthly visits two years ago, Clayton Holdings had quietly started buying wineries. Jack's family now owned four of them.

"I honestly don't know how you're going to make this area something sophisticated people want to visit." Taylor's dress inched up her thighs, but Jack kept his gaze on the traffic. Because the huge oak and maple trees lining the route blazed bright red, orange and yellow, drivers were out in force, enjoying fall color. As Jack took a curve, he slowed, trapped behind a couple seeing the sights. As soon as he got enough open space, he accelerated and passed the older couple enjoying a Saturday afternoon drive.

"This area is great. Look at the trees. Beaumont will be a destination. Even more so than it already is."

The plans were designed and blueprinted. His $100 million vision included an eighteen-hole golf course designed by a master and attached to a resort hotel that would offer world-class spa treatments. He'd purchased land to create a private airstrip that would handle corporate jets. There'd be an enclave of high-end, detached villas for those who wished to own a second or third home with a gorgeous view. Guests could take Missouri River dinner cruises and/or sightseeing excursions on a ninety-six-foot yacht. That plan was one step closer, as Thursday night the county council had approved a plan to expand the local dock. The council had inked a deal with Clayton Holdings—his family company—which would in turn pay a per-person fee to the county. With that complete, Jack had set his sights on expanding the docks of the next two towns over. Eventually maybe he'd add marinas, like those found on the Mississippi River, in what locals called Alton Lake.

For the bicyclists who rode the nearby Katy Trail, which was a rail-to-trail gravel cycling path that ran across most of the state, Jack's vision included paved trails leading from his venues to various trail access points. He'd even have bicycles his guests could rent. He'd also planned wine dinners, tours—the possibilities were endless.

As the convertible devoured the miles out of town, Taylor put her long hair into a ponytail so the wind didn't whip it in her face. Jack allowed himself a quick sideways glance. He knew his parents hoped he'd fall in love with her, but he'd decided it was better for their working relationship to remain platonic. He had zero regrets on that decision.

However, despite making things clear, Jack was pretty sure she still wanted more. When he'd hired her to be his PA, he'd explained he was a workaholic. He'd repeated those words on all their late nights back in the office. She'd arrived in Missouri a week ago and immediately let her displeasure be known. Jack understood. The term Missourians used was Podunk, as in Beaumont was Podunk compared with Portland or San Francisco.

However, as this was the Midwest, no one in Beaumont cared if a bunch of West Coasters thought the state was a backwater or a flyover. Any derision Taylor showed would be met with antipathy. Out here wealth was understated.

As an example, Jack's paternal grandparents still lived in the same small farmhouse they'd always owned.

Jack had several more properties to acquire before the area he and his dad had mapped out would be complete. If all went well, he'd be here a few more months—at most the half a year he'd told Sierra—before he would install a regional manager, allowing Jack to return to Portland. Once Jack finished this job, maybe his dad would finally step aside and name him president instead of VP of Development.

Jack parked in the gravel lot of a two-story, traditional brick farmhouse that had once served guests as the River Bend B&B. Now with its former owners happily retired in Scottsdale, Jack's team had commandeered the building for their offices and residence.

Jack retrieved the cookies and carried them inside. The moment he stepped in the front foyer, he could hear chatter. To his left was a dining room, which now contained a huge conference table covered in empty coffee cups. "I brought cookies!" he called.

"Thank God." Juan Patrick, Clayton Holdings' lead architect for this project rose from where he'd been reviewing topography maps. "I need sugar."

Although Jack tore through the tape and opened the box, Juan's hand went in first. "Oh, these look good." Juan practically moaned his pleasure after he took a bite. "Damn. Worth working six days a week."

"Exactly." Jack reveled in the praise. "See, told you Auntie Jayne's is the best. That's why it's on my list to sign them to a distribution deal."

Jack snagged a cookie before passing the box. "Take one," he urged Taylor. Mildly annoyed with her downturned lip, he broke off a piece of the flatter part of his cookie. "At least try a bite. I want to put these in all my Midwest hotels. What do you think?"

Bright red nails snagged the morsel, which she placed so perfectly that not one speck dared touch her lips. Juan had crumbs everywhere. Will, Jack's on-site attorney and contract guru, returned from the kitchen carrying a couple of empty glasses and a gallon of milk. "Figured it'd save time," Will said, setting everything down.

"Good plan." Jack snagged a glass.

"That's why you hired me," Will joked. "Because I'm proactive."

"Anything happen while we were gone?"

Will wiped his lips on the back of his hand. "We received the counteroffer for Alarcon Vineyards."

"A counter. That's great." At least the Alarcon family hadn't outright rejected the offer of a contract, as had happened with the other winery Jack was pursuing, Jamestown Vineyards.

Will spoke through another bite of cookie. "You might not be thinking it's great when you hear how much they want now that word's gotten out you're the one buying."

Jack poured himself some milk. "They'd be fools not to sell. Their winery won't be profitable once we're up and running, and we're working on that now. We're eight months from breaking ground on the hotel and the golf course should be ready next spring." Jack sat in a leather office chair and gestured with the cookie. There wasn't anything or anyone that couldn't be bought. Most people simply wanted to be heard first. "Show me what they want."

For the next hour, he and Will brainstormed a decent counteroffer, finally deciding on a new price and conditions. Will rose to call their real estate agent and Jack crossed the foyer. Taylor sat in the living room, where they'd arranged several work desks. She glanced up from typing something on her laptop. "Doing okay?" he asked.

"Yes."

He watched her for a moment. "Call went to voice mail," Will yelled from the other room. "I left a message."

"Thanks." Jack approached the five-by-seven-foot satellite-view map of the region. He'd hung the map on the first day they'd moved into the B&B, and he'd marked a red perimeter surrounding the property he wanted. Each time he closed, he'd marked off the property he purchased. Jack took a yellow highlighter and colored in Sunny Days. However, like a half-done jigsaw puzzle, some places inside the red line remained empty. Even though he had hundreds of acres of vines and a slew of historic buildings along Winery Road, he didn't have all the pieces to make the picture and his investment complete.

No, he still had a variety of smaller parcels and a few big ones to purchase, all of which he was working hard to acquire. He took another bite of cookie and wondered if Sierra had baked the ones he'd bought.

Interesting she was back in Beaumont. He'd heard through the grapevine she'd hightailed it for the Naval Academy after high school to follow in her father's footsteps. He wasn't sure, then, why she was baking, minus her parents owning a cookies-only bakery. She appeared healthy. The slim apron had covered a figure that looked fit enough to fly, the flour-covered black accenting a trim waist and curvy hips. Her brown hair had been tamed into a cut longer in the front than the back. She was taller, around five-eight, he figured, since he stood five-eleven, and they'd almost been eye to eye. Her deep brown eyes hadn't changed, minus the hint of a few age lines. He saw the same faint crow's feet in the mirror each morning while he shaved, a consequence of being almost thirty-three. But her expression, had he been wrong in seeing how her eyes had held a glimmer of steely contempt? What was that about? She'd been the one to turn him down flat when he'd asked her out. He put a finger in the middle of the empty space on the map. Or maybe she'd heard he'd made an offer for her parents' winery.

Add that to his list of sins.

He wondered how much she knew about her family's businesses or their finances. He traced his finger over Jamestown Vineyards. The region's pre-

mier winery was home to the perennial state fair
champion Norton, a streak that included the last
three years. Besides the Norton grape, which turned
into the state's famed deep red Norton wine, Jamestown also had a French-American Vignoles grape,
which Marvin James made into a popular drier, yet
semisweet white wine.

Jack had to give the family credit. Marvin was
an expert winemaker and Jayne an expert baker. If
today was any indication, the cookie store thrived.
Although he knew some details from spending half
his life in the area, he'd had Taylor research the family, as Jack would perform due diligence on any potential client or investment.

Marvin had flown in the navy with two of the
town's residents—Mike Thornburg and John Bien—
and on a visit to his friends, he'd met and fallen in
love with Jayne, a woman five years older. Jayne's
family had lived on the vineyard land two generations, so Marvin had moved to Beaumont. With that
much history and longevity of ownership, Marvin
and Jayne would need a good reason to sell. That's
why Jack had made his first offer far lower than he
was willing to pay, but at the same time high enough
as not to insult them right out of the gate. They
hadn't bothered to respond, instead letting the time
run out and expiring the offer. He certainly hadn't
expected zero communication from them.

However, after seeing Sierra today, he realized

he might not have played his hand correctly. He'd considered Sierra out of the equation, but she was back in town and he hadn't known. If Zoe had the cookie store, would Sierra be wanting the winery? Now, before Jack approached Marvin and Jayne again, he required more information. He didn't need any more gaffes.

He'd already made a mistake with Zoe by asking about her husband. Jack stepped away from the map and glanced over to where Taylor typed on her laptop. She'd either missed Zoe's divorce or deemed the fact irrelevant. Taylor had also missed that Sierra was home baking delicious cookies. The box was already half-empty.

It wouldn't help Jack's cause if the next generation wanted to take over. He doubted there were any surprises with Sierra's brothers. Taylor's report said thirty-six-year-old Nelson was an optometrist in the St. Louis suburb of Kirkwood. He had a thriving practice, a wife who worked as a real estate agent and two middle-school-aged kids. Thirty-three-year-old Vance was married to his partner, had a Dalmatian and lived in downtown Chicago, where he worked as a communications executive. Jack expected the James boys to be aware of their parents' businesses, but not involved in the day-to-day operations of either the store or winery.

Sierra was an unexpected variable. Her assessing deep brown eyes, coupled with the way her cheeks had flushed when her gaze had connected with his, had created the same flicker of interest he'd experienced all those years ago in high school, back when he'd been young and dumb. Hell, he'd grown up with her. She'd whipped his butt in sports. She'd kissed him like a house on fire that one time after math tutoring, then rejected him as if he'd been dirt.

"Taylor?" He must have spoken sharply because she stopped typing. "Get me a full dossier on Sierra James."

"The older daughter?"

Jack ignored the disquiet eating his gut. He reminded himself this was business, and business always came first. "Yes. Everything. College. Career. Personal life. Put Anthony on it." Anthony was the investigator Clayton Holdings used. Jack trusted him to be ethical yet efficient.

"I'm sure she'll come up with an internet search but I'll email Anthony like you asked."

"Thank you. Oh, and make that donation to the Halloween festival committee. The level that buys a full-page ad. The back cover of the program if no one's taken it. It was on one of the brochures at the store. We should become more involved in town events so we can show our goodwill and support of the community." After all, Clayton Holdings was here to stay.

As she waited for him to say more, Taylor blinked at him, her lashes perfectly extended and her brow smooth. She was the daughter of a prominent San Francisco athlete, and Jack had met her at a business function he'd attended with his parents. His parents had been the ones to suggest he hire her, and he knew they hoped he and Taylor would be a match. Taylor had a degree in English. He had no idea what Sierra's degree was. Did they give degrees at the Naval Academy? Weren't they mostly engineers? He was behind the curve on this.

He needed to find out everything about Sierra, from her degree to why she was in town and for how long. He calmed his anger at how he'd been such an egotistical high school junior, one who'd failed to contemplate the fact that, just maybe, she didn't like him back, *even* if they'd kissed. His homecoming dance proposal had created all sorts of stupid drama he still didn't understand. He'd thought she'd liked him, but she'd rejected him and never given him the time of day afterward, including the day he'd moved away. The smart play would be to find out what happened and apologize for whatever he did, even if it might be sixteen years after the fact. It was ancient history—but history had a way of affecting the here and now.

And Sierra James sure could affect his here and now.

But knowing Sierra—and seeing how snappily she'd answered him today—he had an instinctive feeling nothing involving her or securing her cooperation would be simple. However, he had to win her over. He couldn't risk having her as an enemy. He needed that land and those vines. The Jameses had to sell. Putting Beaumont County's wine country on the global map, and his future as company president, depended on it. No matter how much Sierra intrigued him, or how she'd sparked his interest—even when wearing a hairnet—Jack would keep his distance.

The deal came first.

Chapter Three

The sun was low on the horizon when Sierra arrived back to her childhood home. She was far later than she'd intended. But she'd stayed extra at the cookie store to talk to Zoe, who seemed somewhat flustered after the new elementary school principal had come in with his daughter. Sierra had told Zoe he'd flirted with her, to which Zoe had insisted that their daughters were friends and if he'd been flirting with her, so had Jack with Sierra.

Once Sierra had extricated herself from that conversation, she'd stopped by the winery to check on things, delighted to find the manager had everything under control. As she drove up the half-mile driveway toward the house, her Chevy Tahoe created an expansive, billowing cloud in its wake. The three-quarter-inch gravel, dry from a week without rain, created a fine dust that covered the dark blue paint with a gritty gray film. She'd run the car though a self-service wash at some point, not that she was fanatical about keeping her car clean, especially as the five-year-old SUV would get dirty again the minute she hit the driveway. Such was life in the country.

Now her plane… That was another story. She still felt the profound loss of seeing it charred, mangled and splintered. She'd cared for her plane as much as her dad did his prized toys, which sat inside a detached four-car garage.

Sierra parked on the expansive concrete pad, her SUV blocking the garage door to bay one. Inside sat her dad's 1978 Corvette C3. Bay two held his favorite baby: an original 1967 Shelby Cobra 427 S/C he'd painstakingly restored and that he'd jokingly called his daughters' inheritance. As she climbed out of her SUV, her dad exited the side door, wiping his hands on a chamois rag.

"Hey, Dad," Sierra called. She pressed the fob to lock the door to the Tahoe, her city-girl habits dying hard. The SUV beeped twice.

He gazed at her a long moment. Then he brightened. "Sierra. Were you out driving?"

She stepped forward to kiss his cheek, which he received with a smile. "I was at the store baking all day."

"Oh yes. Baking. I was polishing. Do you want to see the car?"

"Absolutely." Sierra sensed her mom, and turning, saw her standing on the wide porch that ran along the back side of their traditional, two-story farmhouse. Had her hair turned even grayer than before? She was midsixties. Sierra decided it was a trick of the waning light and gave her mom a wave. "Gonna go look at the car," she called.

"Dinner will be ready in a few. Pot roast," her mom returned, wiping her hands on her apron.

"We'll be ready! I like pot roast," her dad shouted.

"You do," Sierra confirmed, her tone softer. "Always have."

"Your mother." He said the words as if dragging a memory from somewhere. "Your mother always knows pot roast is one of my favorites."

Her dad speed-walked his way into the garage, as quick as ever, and Sierra lengthened her stride to his. The lights blazed, showing off the two classic cars he'd painstakingly restored. The third, a 1964 Chevy Impala SS that Sierra knew would never be finished, sat in bay four with its hood closed. Her dad pointed to the Cobra, which had 22,525 miles on it. "Did I ever tell you how I got this?" he said.

He had, at least hundreds of times before, but Sierra shook her head. "Tell me. I'd love to hear it."

"Back when I was just starting my own body shop, this rich guy came in. Car had some fender damage so he brought it to me. His plan was to fix it and sell it. He just wanted rid of it. He had loads of money. Didn't really care about the car, or how she's a classic. When I saw the chassis number, I made him a fair offer as is and he was like, 'Sold. It'll save me from having to pay you to repair it.'"

Her dad used the chamois cloth and dusted an imaginary spot on the sapphire blue hood. "Only thirty-one of these S/C-tagged babies. Still runs like a champ. Shall we take it out for a spin?"

"Not today," Sierra replied. Her dad hadn't driven in years, not since his diagnosis of early-onset Alzheimer's. "Jayne made pot roast and it's ready."

Not quite sixty until Christmas Eve, the disease made her dad's brain act like one far older. "I think I like pot roast."

"You do, and it will get cold if we wait too long," Sierra replied. "No one likes cold pot roast."

"No, they don't," he agreed.

They left the garage, and Sierra locked the door and set the alarm. As she closed the door behind them, her dad saw her parked SUV. "Were you out driving today to see the fall color?"

"Yes, Dad. I was."

"And you like the Tahoe? It handles well?"

"I do." She smiled at him, her heart hurting. When she'd returned home two months ago, she'd discovered her mom had kept the full extent of her dad's early-onset Alzheimer's disease a secret from her, citing "you had your own issues to handle."

Her mom meant Sierra's PTSD, which mainly manifested itself as a fear of flying. For a year following the crash, Sierra had worked with doctors to get better, but even when she'd managed to get into the flight simulator, she'd frozen. Had a panic attack. Crashed again, the ground rising to meet her before she could even jettison from the cockpit.

Unable to fly, after extensive discussions with her superiors, Sierra had requested an honorable discharge instead of reassignment, and the navy had let her go. She'd planned to be a lifer. Earn ranks beyond lieutenant.

Instead she'd returned home. Found she was needed there because her former navy pilot, turned body shop owner, turned winemaker dad—her hero—was losing the battle with a disease that would rob him of his mind and memory and, eventually, his life.

From the outside, he appeared so young—his hair finally turning full gray. It simply wasn't fair, and Sierra thanked God her mom was in good health, especially considering Jayne James was doing double duty taking care of her husband and running the family's two businesses.

The three of them settled around the kitchen table. Today was a good day for her dad, as his word deficiencies weren't as noticeable. His disease meant that, besides the pronounced forgetfulness, forks often became "that thing you eat with" and airplanes "that thing I used to fly."

Her dad still knew people's names, he still recognized his family even if it took a second or two, and he didn't miss a beat when winemaking and tending to his vines. He'd gotten positive results from taking part in an experimental drug trial. However, as he continued on the medication, he'd plateaued. Sometimes it seemed as if he was getting worse.

"How was the store?" her mom asked. For years the cookie store had been how her mom had kept her fingers on the pulse of Beaumont, and she'd turned over the entire operation to Zoe in July.

"Sales were brisk. Zoe's doing a great job with everything."

"I'm glad." Her mom reached to wipe some brown gravy off the side of her dad's mouth. "I miss it, though. Seeing who came in. The few times a week I get there when Dad's at his center always go by so fast."

"Jack Clayton came in. You know, the one who asked me to homecoming."

Her mom frowned. "You turned him down, if I remember. Said you didn't like him and you weren't going just to go."

"I did." Sierra hadn't told her mom the entire story, only telling her best friend, Emily, and Zoe. "He said he's bought Elephant Rock and Primrose

Hill." Sierra took a bite of whipped potatoes and frowned. "You don't seem surprised by that."

Her mom picked at the paper napkin. "There was an article in the paper. He has big plans. One is to buy this place. We received an offer from Clayton Holdings. We let it expire."

The delicious potatoes turned into chalky paste and Sierra washed them down with her mom's sweetened iced tea. "He made an offer for the winery? Why didn't you tell me?"

Her mom didn't appear concerned. "There was nothing to tell. Like I said, we let it expire."

"What's this about the winery expiring?" Her dad engaged into the conversation.

"The offer to buy it," her mom said.

"Someone made an offer?" her dad asked. "We just sold the body shop. I'm looking forward to making wine. Norton. My favorite kind. Did you know the Norton grape is considered a native grape? It was crossbred in Virginia by Dr. Daniel Norton, and the vine first appeared in Missouri in 1830. But after Prohibition it took until 1989 before it started being grown again in large quantities. Now the Norton/Cynthiana grape, or *Vits Aestivalis*, is the state grape. That happened in 2003."

Unable to handle how her dad could recite miscellaneous facts about grapes but not remember that he'd sold the body shop ten years ago, Sierra rose and cleared her dinner plate. She returned with a stack of dessert plates. Then she retrieved the two-layer cake her mom had baked and cut a huge slice. She took a bite of what could only be described as much-needed chocolate therapy. "This is good."

"You could cut two more pieces," her mom pointed out. "We're finished eating now too."

"Ooh, the dark kind. My favorite." Her dad reached out with his dinner knife and began to cut a chunk from the cake.

Her mom wore a bemused smile as she watched the chunk flop onto Marvin's dessert plate. Her mom deserved a sainthood award, Sierra thought. Dealing with her husband's illness and running the businesses couldn't be easy. And Jack wanted to buy Jamestown? The gall of the man.

"I'd like to see this offer, if I can," Sierra said.

"It's electronic and I already deleted the email that linked to it," her mom said with a dismissive wave of her fork. "Your sister-in-law looked at it. She said it certainly wasn't worth accepting. Way under value."

Which raised the question, if Jack made a better offer, would her parents consider selling? "Well, you let me know if another one comes in. I'm here now. I can help out more. Just say the word."

"While that's lovely, I've got this. You have an engineering degree and a standing offer from Boeing, one you still haven't accepted. Don't let that expire." Her mom harped on Sierra's future in that tone that said, "Take the job." Sierra fidgeted as her mom wiped away some loose crumbs.

"Got what?" her dad reengaged with them in between bites of cake. He wore a smear of chocolate on his face. "How's flying?" he asked Sierra.

When she'd first moved home, she'd tried to explain to her dad she no longer flew for the navy. He hadn't understood. Or remembered.

"Marvin, let the girl eat her cake without you pestering her. And you're wearing icing on your chin again." Her mom used a light and teasing tone, but Sierra swore she heard underlying weariness.

Her dad, however, laughed and cleaned his face before digging his fork back into the cake for another delicious bite, as no one baked like Sierra's mom. Dinner ended on a lighter note, as her mom and dad critiqued classic television shows, which they still watched courtesy of the satellite dish installed on the side of the house.

After helping her mom load dishes and clean the kitchen, Sierra headed upstairs. The second step gave her a good view of the back of her dad's head; he sat in front of the seventy-inch flat-screen TV watching a 1980s concert of one of his favorite bands, the channel logo visible in the lower right corner of the screen. She climbed the rest of the way, her tennis shoes thudding against the hardwood. The original portion of the second floor dated back to 1830 and consisted of two oversize bedrooms.

The modern addition off the back added two more bedrooms and three bathrooms, including the owners' suite.

Before the expansion, Sierra and her sister had shared a bedroom in the front of the house, in the historic part, with her two older brothers sharing the other front room. Now those two connecting rooms had been converted into a playroom and child's bedroom for Zoe's daughter, used whenever Megan spent the night. A hall bathroom serviced those rooms.

Sierra had moved into the guest bedroom, which had its own bathroom. Painted a pleasant, soft gray with white bedding and curtains, the room offered a view that overlooked her mom's huge vegetable garden and the acre-sized pond beyond. Minus unpacking her suitcases and hanging up her clothes, Sierra had done nothing to personalize the space. Most of her prized possessions remained in moving boxes that she'd stored in the newer portion of the walk-out basement. The utilitarianism of the space suited her. She wasn't planning on staying home forever, so the not-personal space reminded her this move wasn't permanent.

Then again, at the same time she couldn't let her mom do this alone. Zoe had enough on her plate with raising Megan and running the store. Her brothers had high-pressure careers. Sierra refused to shirk her family responsibilities. Deciding what to do about the job offer could wait for now.

She retrieved her phone and performed a Google search before sending a quick text to her best friend, Emily: You won't believe who came into the store today. Sierra's phone rang instead of her receiving a texted reply. "Hey."

"Do not tell me it's Jerk Clayton. The audacity of that man to come back here," Emily greeted.

Sierra sighed. "How'd you know?"

"I saw his picture in the paper, and seriously, of course it's him because only one man in the universe has ever gotten you into this type of a tizzy. What did he do now?"

"He bought a dozen cookies. I don't think he knew I was back. Or maybe it was seeing me in my Auntie Jayne's uniform that shocked him."

"Ouch. Those are not flattering."

Sierra imagined Emily's wince and mirrored it with one of her own. "Yeah, tell me about it. I've always imagined seeing him again. I'd be all hot and gorgeous and he'd be full of regret and he'd tell me he was sorry, and I'd be like too bad, it's too late, loser. Instead I was in a hairnet with flour covering my apron and sprinkles on my shirt."

"I'm sorry, girlfriend. That sucks. But how does he look? All I've seen are the pictures in the paper."

"Far too handsome for his own good. He was

with some blonde. You know the kind that money drips from."

"Yeah, I do their injections and chemical peels." Emily was a board-certified dermatologist. Half of her thriving practice in the outskirts of St. Louis County consisted of cosmetic procedures. "He looks that good, huh?"

As an outlet for nervous tension, Sierra fingered the bedspread without even realizing she was doing it. "Am I that pathetic or hard up that seeing him made my stomach flutter? In high school, the guy asked me out because of a bet." She refused to broach the subject of that one time she and Jack had kissed during math tutoring. "And now he's trying to buy my parents' winery. I should not be like, ooh, he's hot, take me, I'm yours, you gorgeous hunk of a man."

"Damn. That good-looking."

"Yeah. I actually got tingles." Sierra smoothed out the spot. "I keep telling myself the fantasy is always better than the reality. Sometimes the gift wrap is the best part of the present. He might look great, but he's still a disappointing jerk."

"There you go, being all profound and peppy. Tells me how much his surprise arrival shook you. No worries. You got this. He's not worth it."

"Of course he's not." Sierra stood, went to the window and gazed out over the dark backyard. "He's not going to get the best of me again."

"If he tries, he'll have me to deal with. Hey, how about we do late dinner this week? I see my last patients at five, so I could meet you around six thirty and we can have one of our sit-and-gripes. Jeff can watch the kids. I need some me time with my bestie, more than our Monday breakfasts. I almost spoke to one of my patients as if they were a child today."

Emily had three-year-old twin boys who'd turn four in January. Sierra adored them but they were energetic whirlwinds. "We've got a monthly wine dinner this upcoming Thursday. I can snag us two spots. Got an in with the owner."

Emily laughed. "I'd sure hope so. I'm entering dinner into my calendar now. I will be there come hell or high water. Speaking of my beloved handfuls, it's bath time, so I have to run. See you for breakfast."

With that, Emily ended the call. Sierra set her phone down and smiled. Emily always cheered her up. They were self-proclaimed "sisters from different mothers" and friends for two and a half decades. Emily had done a six-year medical program at the University of Missouri–Kansas City, where she'd also met her husband. Five years ago, Sierra had taken leave and stood in as Emily's maid of honor. If anyone deserved to have it all, it was Emily.

Sierra had a winery shift tomorrow afternoon, so she made a mental note to remember to tell the hostess to reserve two places. She glanced at the bedside clock. The over-twenty-one crowd of college students would be starting to hit the bars on the northern end of Main Street, ready to find adventure, fun and maybe love, even if just for the night. Once she'd been young and adventurous too, although the navy had stricter rules than River Bend, a small liberal arts school located on the northern end of Beaumont.

Tonight she was older, wiser and tired. And, 5:00 a.m. came too early—she'd never been able to reset her body clock from her favorite early morning running time. She still retained many of the habits ingrained from her years in the service. One was reading her way to sleep. Sierra retrieved the nonfiction book on thermodynamics, pulled out the bookmark and settled in. She refused to wonder what Jack was doing, or with whom.

She wanted nothing from Jack except to give him an earful. Her parents' winery was off-limits. He'd messed with her once. She was no longer a naive girl with stars in her eyes over the fact that maybe, just maybe, one of the most popular guys in school liked her, only to learn it was all a lie.

He'd rue the day he messed with her, or her family, again.

Chapter Four

Because the unseasonably warm October weather meant guests could sit outside in long sleeves and light jackets, the tasting room and seating areas at Sierra's family winery were nonstop busy Sunday afternoon. The Great Room, where Sierra worked behind the bar, also doubled as Jamestown Vineyards' dining room. Modeled on the lobby of the Tenyana Hotel at Yosemite, the Great Room was a huge, open expanse with two-story-high ceilings, dark wooden trusses and rustic chandeliers.

Unlike the smaller tasting rooms of neighboring wineries, Jamestown's was built so the length of the gigantic room was double the width. A wall full of two-story-high windows stood opposite the front doors, providing a sweeping view of rolling hills.

Guests could stop at the long bar running along the entire left side, or they could head outside onto the huge deck, where a duo played music. When looking right from inside the front doors, the room had an eight-foot-wide floor-to-ceiling stone fireplace. On cold days, Jamestown kept a roaring fire going.

"I need another glass of Norton and two white blends," Kate called as she approached the wait stand. Sierra liked working with the twenty-two-year-old who was in her final year at River Bend College. "They've already been through two glasses each. Would have been cheaper to buy a bottle but they couldn't decide on a vintage. I think they're on a first date and didn't think they'd like each other that much."

"More proof dating sucks, but at least it helps our bottom line." Sierra reached into the cooler for the white blend and filled two new glasses as Kate keyed in the order.

After Kate left, Sierra took a minute to assess the crowd. All the tables were occupied, with scant few open seats available at the bar. Jamestown served a full menu until its 5:00 p.m. closing time. The chef created stacked charcuterie boards with specialty cured meats and handcrafted cheeses, salads and a variety of hot or cold gourmet sandwiches that came with either chips or fries.

"Oops, sorry." The head bartender skirted around Sierra's backside.

"No worries," Sierra called after him as Jerry reached for a bottle of Chambourcin, a wine made from a purple-skinned, French-American hybrid grape. While not as popular as her dad's Norton, the Chambourcin fermented in steel, giving it a light body with hints of tart cherry, dried cranberry and a fresh herb finish. Jerry poured glasses for a group of four who'd decided not to wait for table service.

Kate returned to the wait stand and caught Sierra's attention. "Can you bring this Vignoles out to table sixty-five? They already have glasses." Kate mouthed, "Emergency. I'll need to take five."

Sierra understood perfectly. "Jerry? I'll be right back. Bar's yours."

"Got it," Jerry called, his attention on the customers in front of him.

With the bar covered, Sierra filled a white plastic bucket with ice and added a sealed bottle of Vignoles. Grabbing a wine opener, she headed outside. A fresh fall breeze caressed her face as she exited the Great Room. She inhaled a deep breath of earthy air so different from the salty aroma of Pensacola.

The duo's cover of John Denver's "Take Me Home Country Roads" mingled with guests' conversation as Sierra wove her way through the tables. Table sixty-five was at the far end of the deck, around a slight dogleg. The four-top contained three men and a woman—who was wearing designer sunglasses Sierra recognized. Stomach plummeting, Sierra forced a smile onto her face. Was he stalking her family's property to figure out a new approach? She set the bucket on the table, making certain the white plastic didn't thump or the ice splash. Even though she'd vowed to let Jack have it next time she saw him, she wouldn't make a scene here, any more than she would at the cookie store.

"Sierra?"

She ignored the friendly smile Jack bestowed. "Kate's on a short break. I'm here to open your wine." Sierra withdrew the bottle from the bucket, careful not to drip water. Deep down, part of her craved a tiny bit of revenge by covering Jack's blue polo and khakis with water droplets. After all, they'd dry. But Sierra remained the ultimate professional. She uncorked the wine, something servers did at the table to prove to their guests that no one drank from their bottle but them. She poured a sample into his glass and waited.

He lifted the glass, swirled and sipped. "As good as the first bottle."

As if there would be any doubt. She filled their glasses, observing those with him. She didn't recognize the two men, who were dressed similarly to Jack. The woman wore a short sundress as if she were in Beverly Hills instead of rural Missouri. Sierra shoved the bottle back in the ice and grabbed the bucket containing the empty bottle. "Kate will check on you in a few."

Carrying the bucket high, she wove her way back to the bar.

Not even five minutes later, Jack slid into an empty seat in front of her. "Hey."

Sierra's heart jumped and she squashed her excitement. Sure he was handsome, and what woman didn't like the attention of an attractive man? However, she knew him too well. "Something wrong with the wine?"

"No. The wine's great. You're not baking cookies today."

"Obviously." Purposely not looking at him lest the part of her that found him attractive win, she passed a bottle of Jamestown's red blend to a server. When Jack didn't move, Sierra relented. "Did you need something?"

"Came to talk to you. We didn't get a chance to do that yesterday." Jack gave her what seemed to be a genuine smile, one she'd long ago wished he'd permanently direct her way. Today the full wattage of that disarming smile created magic, and she tried to ignore the tingles running through her.

"You're assuming I want to talk to you. Can't you see I'm busy?"

His intense gaze never wavered. "Too busy to spare a minute for an old friend?"

Was he being clever or did he actually think they were friends? Time to curtail both. "Is that what we are? Or are you the person who lowballed my parents in an attempt to steal this place away from them?"

His nod conveyed an immediate grasp of the situation. "Ah, the reason for the open hostility you're currently sending my direction."

Her worst habit was rolling her eyes, but she couldn't help herself. "It was an insulting offer. This place is not for sale—ever—so while you can come and enjoy the wine—I can't stop you—don't sit here at my bar and get grand ideas. Your credit card payment is the only money my family wants. Why are you here anyway? Don't you have enough wineries? Wouldn't you be better off patronizing one of them? Pad your bottom line?"

He had the gall to chuckle. "Nah. I know all about those. It's the ones I don't own I'm interested in. What's great about them? What's temperamental? What's perfect the way it is? I'm willing to put in the work necessary to make a relationship work."

Like a heat-seeking missile, she couldn't tear her gaze away. Was he still talking about wineries? Or... something else entirely?

She could figure out military games, but not the kind that dealt with the heart. At least this time she wasn't wearing a hairnet, but rather a T-shirt with the winery name and a pair of jeans.

She regrouped and attacked another flank. "Then shouldn't you be overseeing or something? Oh, wait. Never mind. I'm sure you have people for that."

That devastating grin became a bemused smile, and Sierra didn't know whether to be insulted or relieved he'd ignored her deliberate rudeness. He drummed his fingers idly on the polished oak, making no move to leave the bar. "Still the same spirited spitfire as you were in high school. Glad to see some things haven't changed."

She raised both brows. "Oh, hardly. I'm much more deadly."

A small, amused shake of his head accompanied his "If you say so. It's rather hot, you know, the way your chest puffs like that when you're trying to score a point."

"I…" She was going to kill him. Slowly. With her bare hands. That or do something stupid and act on the sexual tension suddenly zinging like loose electrons.

His wink revealed he knew he'd gotten under her skin. "And before you go all high and mighty on me, we kept all the management and workers on-site of everything we purchased. Everything remained status quo. No one lost their jobs unless they wanted to receive a severance package."

She had to give him some credit for that. Sort of. "I did some online research on you, last night, after I found out you're trying to acquire this place too. You're gobbling up everything."

He put a hand over his left pectoral, one that would feel delightful under her fingers. "Oh, Sierra, be still my heart. I was worried you didn't care. You could have just asked. I'm an open book. I'll tell you everything you want to know. Just say the word and I'm all yours."

She'd cough "bullshit" but she was thirty, not eighteen. Zoe had been right yesterday at the store. He was flirting with her. He really was a cad, wasn't he? How dare he flirt and flatter after what he'd done in high school. She exaggerated an annoyed breath. "Ha. Always the comedian. I'm surprised you have people willing to sit and break bread with you."

"Now who's a comedian? That's my architect, my attorney and my PA. You might have seen her the other day in the store."

"That makes sense." Now she knew who the blonde was. Sierra grabbed a rag and wiped down the bar top. "You pay them. They have to pretend to like you and the monstrosities you're building."

"Har, har," he scoffed. "You always were witty with words. One of the things I liked about you. Good to see that's still the same. As for the wineries, we'll make sure all the changes fit into the environment. We brought in a horticulturalist to make sure we do things right when we remove any trees."

Sierra didn't register the part about trees as much as the part where he'd said he liked her. His words had given her the warm fuzzies. "Did you need something or is this more of an exercise in figuring out how to waste more of my time? Another bottle? Perhaps you could order some food?"

"Food," he decided. "Send over an order of toasted ravioli and some spinach-artichoke dip."

"Done." Sierra swiped her card against one of the computers and typed in an order of spinach and artichoke dip and an order of toasted ravioli, a St. Louis invention, and set both for delivery to table sixty-five. "Added to your tab. Anything else?" She folded her arms across her chest, desensitizing breasts that itched for his touch.

Jack studied her for a long moment. "You've really changed, haven't you?"

His scrutiny made her feel uncomfortable, as if she was the one who'd done something wrong instead of the bet he'd made at her expense. "If you mean being able to stand on my own two feet, yeah. The navy sort of teaches you how to do that before you take charge of a billion-dollar aircraft."

Pensive creases formed in his forehead but otherwise he appeared relaxed and unaffected. What was that saying in business? Never let them see you sweat? He'd clearly mastered that art. "Look, whatever I did…"

"Is irrelevant." She wasn't delving into that topic, not today. Not ever. "Scratch this place off your list and we'll call it even."

Jack shoved his hands into his front pockets. She jerked her gaze upward. "How about I show you what I'm doing? Let you see my plans? Give you a full tour?"

Her curiosity spiked. Not that she'd let him know about that. "I'm not interested."

He dangled a carrot. "Think of it as a way to scope out the competition. An insider look. A way to learn my secrets. Even if I don't buy this winery, you're going to be competing with the ones I have bought."

True. His offer tempted, especially considering what she'd read about his ambitious plans. While her parents made a decent profit on this winery, there was still a mortgage to pay, vines to tend and employees to pay. If Jack monopolized everything so that Jamestown was the only family enterprise left, his actions could cut into the bottom line.

There was an adage that if something wasn't green and growing, it was ripe and rotting. Jamestown Vineyards had always had the region's most innovative ideas. Wineries were as much about the experience as the wine, which was why Jamestown offered wine by the glass and table service. Most Beaumont wineries had one tiny tasting counter and sold prepackaged food out of self-service refrigerators. Jamestown's Great Room dwarfed most places, and the complete menu had set new standards. Now, because of her dad's disease, the winery rested on past laurels—perfectly content in the atmosphere they'd so carefully cultivated. Instead of thinking up new business innovations, her dad concentrated on tending his vines, something he instinctively knew how to do no matter how bad his dementia. With the skilled manager her family had in place, though, she saw no reason things couldn't continue as they were for the foreseeable future. Minus the fact that Jack Clayton threatened to upend everything. Darn it. Reconnaissance was always beneficial in combat, especially when it was safe to do.

"Fine," she agreed. "I'll listen to your sales pitch. Only because this is my family's legacy and I want to be prepared to defend it. But I'm excellent at resisting the hard sell. No timeshares in my portfolio."

"Fair enough." The hint of a satisfied smile playing about his lips made her wonder if she'd made a mistake. Had she underestimated him? "Shall we say around eleven tomorrow? Or do you have to work either here or at Auntie Jayne's?"

The winery served customers Wednesdays through Sundays, starting at eleven. The cookie store opened daily at eleven and closed at six. Tomorrow was her day off. "I can make that work. Where shall I meet you?"

"I'll come get you unless you're afraid to ride in my car with me."

There were a lot of things she was afraid of, but her gut said riding in a car alone with Jack wasn't one of them. "I'm temporarily staying with my parents."

"Entrance off Route F, right?"

The James homestead was on the total opposite end of the acreage from the winery tasting room, or as her dad used to say, two miles the way the crow flies. "Yes."

Jack gave her a genuinely pleased smile, not the charming one he dispensed with ease. Sierra felt the impact down to her toes. "Then I'll pick you up at eleven. Jeans are fine, plus good walking shoes. Hope you're not afraid of getting a little dirty."

The wrong image jumped into her head, one of her and Jack tangled on a bed. Sierra blinked to disengage the vision, and as she did, she saw the blonde who worked with Jack squeeze into the wedge of space between Jack and the person seated on the barstool to his left.

"Here you are." Taylor—that was her name, Sierra remembered. Taylor's gaze flickered over Sierra but didn't linger. Not that Sierra expected Taylor to consider her a significant threat, even if she had recognized Sierra from the cookie shop. Women like Taylor didn't see or acknowledge those they deemed beneath their notice, and yesterday Sierra had been in apron and hairnet.

As if already bored with standing at the bar, Taylor placed her hand lightly on Jack's forearm, her fingertips curling slightly. "The food we ordered is on the table. If you want some before Will and Juan eat it all, you best get out there."

"I'll be right there." However, instead of taking

his words as a dismissal, Taylor remained in place. But Sierra had moved during the interaction, taking the opportunity to step toward the server station and out of Jack's electromagnetic orbit.

"Sierra, I need two bottles of Norton." Kate approached the wait stand.

"Coming right up." Sierra turned her back on Jack and grabbed the wine. When she pivoted, she experienced both relief and disappointment to see his extremely nice backside walking toward his outdoor table. Taylor followed him on three-inch heels.

Sierra handed Kate the bottles. "Do you know him?" Kate asked as she swiped her plastic access card.

"That's Jack Clayton. We went to high school together. He was two grades ahead of me."

"Well, he's pretty handsome for an older guy. Still got it going. You should go for that."

Sierra covered the racing of her heart with a fast protest. "Hey. I'm two years younger than him. Thirty is not old."

Then again, when she'd been Kate's age, thirty had sounded over the hill. Now Sierra crept on being thirty-one in March. Time sure did seem to fly—New Year's Eve was ten weeks away. Sierra frowned. If she said yes, her employment with Boeing would start January 3. The company wanted the entire team fully engaged by mid-January.

Kate took the bottles in hand and went off to

serve table sixty-one. "No worries. You still got it going on."

"Nice save," Sierra called after her. Grinning, Sierra turned her attention to the next order. By five thirty, the crowds had thinned, especially once the music ended. The winery technically closed at five, but in reality that's when the kitchen and bar stopped serving. There would be stragglers sitting around until about six thirty, the outliers staying to watch the sunset and sober up before heading home.

Sierra couldn't blame them for wanting to eke out the last vestiges of fall. After daylight saving time ended, the offseason officially began and the large crowds disappeared until mid-March. Sure, a smattering would come spend a lazy indoor afternoon. Jamestown had a few weddings booked, and the winery always sold out its monthly seven-course dinner evenings, like the one she and Emily would attend Thursday. Wine club members would pick up their monthly allotment. But for the most part, the place was dead. The winery made most of its profits from walk-ins who visited June to October. Auntie Jayne's Cookies saw most of its walk-in traffic during the holidays and/or the two weekends in September when Main Street held its annual fall craft festival and then its famed hot-air balloon race.

"Has table sixty-five closed out?" she asked Kate. From this vantage point, Sierra couldn't see Jack's location.

Kate placed used wineglasses into a rack for washing while Sierra did the opposite. She unloaded clean glasses so they'd be ready to go next Wednesday. "Yeah, about an hour ago."

Sierra released some of the tension she'd been holding in her shoulders. She'd wondered if he'd approach her again, but realistically, why should he? While Sierra didn't consider her appearance shabby, she wasn't the glamorous Taylor with her designer heels. Sierra wore aviators, not Dolce and Gabbana. Levi's, not Frame jeans.

Sierra gave herself a little shake. She shouldn't be wanting Jack's attention. She lifted the empty dish tub, raised it overhead and stacked it on the pile behind the bar. She turned around to see Jack standing there. Her heart gave a leap. "You closed your tab. I thought you'd left." She managed to control her wince. *Dumb, Sierra, dumb. Don't let him know you were thinking about him.*

He slid onto the stool. "We weren't ordering anything else, so I wanted to free up your wait staff."

That was thoughtful. Darn the man for having one good quality. He should be horrible through and through. Live up to the jerk nickname she'd assigned him. "Where are your friends?"

"I had a lunch meeting, so we drove separately. They've left."

Sierra absorbed that. He'd sent Taylor on ahead.

She wouldn't assume it meant anything. "Well, don't let me keep you."

Broad shoulders shrugged. "I don't have anywhere I have to be. Can I help out?"

"You want to clean?" Disbelieving, she searched his face. Surely he was joking.

His hands gestured a show of surrender. "Why not? I own a bunch of wineries now. I should do the nitty-gritty. Isn't that what you insinuated earlier? That I need to work? Immerse myself?"

Sierra stared at him, realizing he was serious. "I'm not going to get rid of you, am I?"

"Not easily." Jack's charming smile disarmed, and part of her relented.

Two people would make the chores go faster, Sierra rationalized. And if he got his precious loafers scuffed while doing trash duty, that was not her problem. He'd volunteered. She ignored the voice warning her she was forgetting her vow to let him have it, or to avoid him at all costs. "Fine. You can help. Follow me."

Chapter Five

She'd agreed to let him stay and help. Sitting on the patron side of the bar, Jack waited and watched while she finished one last chore before indicating he should follow her. Relief and male satisfaction mixed with unfamiliar excitement. He'd wondered if she'd reject him again but figured why not try?

Story of his life—rejection from Sierra James.

Earlier today, when he met his coworkers here, he'd wondered if she'd be on-site. He'd visited Jamestown multiple times over the past year, as he had with every other winery in Beaumont. Today, however, he'd experienced an odd sense of hopeful anticipation once he and his crew had firmed up plans to go to Jamestown. When she'd delivered their wine, his earlier wondering bloomed into opportunity. He'd also experienced lust—her jeans showed off legs that would make a dead man salivate. Jack had once thought her cute. Now she was stunning. His attraction was that of a hummingbird to sugar water. He flitted about, wanting more and more.

"When did you move back?" he asked Sierra as they fell into step. She had a long stride that he easily matched.

"About two months ago. Why did you start buying wineries?"

In high school she'd been blunt, clever and direct. He found himself glad some things hadn't changed. "Blame my parents. They've decided they're retiring here, well, at least for part of the year. They saw this venture as an opportunity to bring everything they loved about Oregon's Willamette Valley back to their roots. My paternal grandparents never left."

The square set of her shoulders said she wasn't too impressed. As if holding back a reply, she bit her lower lip before letting go with a pop. "I'm about to start collecting the empty bottles. Just because we put boxes next to trash cans doesn't mean people follow directions or know where to put their empties."

She'd sped up, and he adjusted his step. "You have a brisk, efficient walk."

"Comes from striding across the tarmac. When you're out on a carrier, it can be windy. You don't lollygag. You can keep up, can't you?"

"Of course I can. I'm no wimp."

They reached an outdoor storage shed. She opened the door, reached inside and yanked the handle of an empty Gorilla cart. Pulling the four-wheeled cart behind her like a practiced expert, she set two corrugated wine boxes and a large black trash bag inside. "You coming?"

"Still trying to get rid of me?"

She rolled her eyes and took off. They headed toward one of the far, grassy areas where bottles re-mained on tables. Jack knew better than to offer to take the cart in some misguided and unwanted show of chauvinism. He did, however, jump in and start retrieving empty bottles the moment they reached them.

"Do you do this all the time?" He set three bot-tles into the first box.

"When it's a family business, everyone pitches in. I've been retrieving bottles since my dad opened. Since I've come home, I bounce between here and the cookie store depending on where I'm needed. It simply depends on the day."

"I see," Jack said, although he really didn't. After a career in the navy, did she really want to be a win-ery employee? He dug deeper for more. "In my or-ganization, winery managers are full-time. Same for my chef. Yours?"

"Of course. When my dad first opened, he was always on-site. He believed that an owner pitched in just as hard as his employees, maybe even more so. It sets a good example. Now he's more behind the scenes."

"Are you wanting to run the winery full-time now that you're back?"

She gave him side-eye. "Trying to find out why we won't take your offer? Is that why you're hanging out with me collecting bottles?"

"Partly," Jack admitted, because he'd long ago learned that, with Sierra, only honesty would do. "I'm also genuinely curious. You talked nonstop about planes. Like Shelby Bien, you took flying lessons. The school paper did an article on you both."

"She's Shelly Thornburg now. And thanks for making me sound like one of those people who peaked too early."

"That's not what I meant. I was going to play professional soccer. You see how that turned out."

"You were always going to take over your parents' company and I'm in between jobs. I've got an offer from Boeing, but the position doesn't start until the new year. I'm still weighing my options."

"Boeing's a great company." The aerospace giant had come into the region decades ago when it purchased McDonnell Douglas. Over twelve thousand fighter jets had been built in St. Louis in the seventy-five-plus years. "So will you be working on fighter jets?"

"Boeing is building the F-15EX for the air force.

It also builds the F/A-18, space and missile systems and the T-7 Red Hawk, which is the air force's new pilot training system."

She'd avoided his question. "I could get that from Google. What's your job?"

"Something in engineering. I don't know if I'm taking it. Ask me when I do."

She reached for a bottle, upended it and dumped out any remaining liquid. Then she set the bottle right side up inside one of the box slots. Jack mimicked her actions and several minutes later they had the tables cleared. The bottles rattled as Sierra pulled the cart back toward the main buildings. On the horizon, the last vestiges of daylight slipped from the sky, leaving slivers of orange and red along the horizon.

Jack took it in. "The view is incredible."

"I'll agree with you on that."

The doors to a metal building stood open. Once inside, Jack helped Sierra stack the boxes next to others already filled. "Are you recycling?"

"Actually, we'll have them professionally washed and sterilized so we can reuse them," Sierra said. "My dad got the idea from some of the dairies who sell their milk in glass bottles and he decided to try it here."

"That's a great idea. Your dad's always been a forward thinker."

"They're starting to reuse bottles in Europe and Oregon. You haven't seen it where you are?"

He shook his head. "No, but I'm going to discuss the idea with my dad."

"A wine bottle can be used up to seven times, and it's cheaper to wash and purify them than to recycle. We do buy new bottles because we have no control over the people who take them home, but reusing our own glass whenever we can not only saves money but also reduces our carbon footprint. It's not enough to get a Climate Neutral Certification, but we're working on that. We've even worked on reducing the weight of our bottles and composting our food waste."

"I'm going to look into this." None of the wineries he'd bought reused their bottles or composted, which now seemed short-sighted.

The dusk-to-dawn lights flickered on, and solar lights cast a soft glow over the pathway. It was a lovely temperate night and Jack didn't want to leave her company, not when he was finally getting to spend time with her. Maybe that made him foolish, but he'd always liked how he felt when he was with her, at least until their final interactions. He didn't want to wait until tomorrow to get to know her better, to see whom she'd become. "What are you doing after this? Let me take you to dinner," Jack offered.

"Why? I'm already meeting you tomorrow." She folded her arms across her chest, hiding the name of the winery that crossed the T-shirt. "Eleven hundred hours. My house."

Not quite a Sierra James rejection. "Tomorrow I'm going to show you around and tell you my plans and talk business. Tonight the only wine I want to discuss is whatever we decide to drink for dinner, if we choose to drink any."

He liked how her eyebrows quirked. "You want more wine?"

"I was making a point that I don't want to talk shop." Sixteen years vanished in an instant. He wanted to kiss her under the soft lights that surrounded them and find out if her mouth was as sweet as he remembered. Yeah, he was a fool still around her.

"What would we have to talk about?"

"The food? The weather? The past sixteen years?" He hoped he didn't sound like a lovestruck fool desperate for a minute of his crush's time. He really had to get his act together. "You have to eat, don't you? Miller's Grill shouldn't be crowded and we can be in and out. You'll save me from microwaving one of those frozen meals. My companions ate all the food I ordered. And this way, if you hate me by the end of our time tomorrow, we'll at least have had one civilized nonbusiness meal."

"Civilized, huh? You think you can manage that?" His libido gave a jolt as Sierra nibbled her lower lip. "Okay," she said finally. "And before you think I'm caving to your charm, I'm agreeing only because my mom serves leftovers every Sunday night and I don't feel like eating pot roast two nights in a row. I'll meet you there. Oh, and Jack?"

"Yeah?"

She shot him a wicked grin that went straight to his groin. "I know you want me to wait until the end of the day tomorrow to decide, but what's to say I don't hate you already?"

Sierra might not like him trying to buy her parents' winery, but he'd bet all his money she didn't hate him.

Far from it.

Chapter Six

As she walked next to Jack toward the parking lot, Sierra couldn't believe she'd told him that maybe she already hated him. If the silly bouncy balls going haywire in her stomach were any indication, *hate* wasn't the word. But after she landed her zinger about hating him, Sierra knew that even if she'd wounded him, he'd never let on.

Instead he laughed, as if the barb had been no more than a gnat to shoo away. "Good one. You know what they say. It's a fine line between love and hate. Tell me, do you color inside the lines or out?"

"You're funny." He was also hot as hell, with a low and smooth voice that enticed her to give in to temptation and find out how well he made love. The moment of heightened sexual tension stretched, and as if some form of cosmic payback, the overhead parking lights somehow made the infernal man look even sexier, the dancing light and flitting shadows deepening those arresting dimples and making his hair even more glossy and finger worthy.

"Well," he finally drawled out in no-holds-barred innuendo that gave her goose bumps, "I'm going to do everything I can to change your mind about hating me. I'll see you at Miller's."

Before Sierra could launch another retort to regain some ground, such as "I'll never change my mind," he slid into an envy-worth Mercedes convertible and sped off. Figured he'd have a sleek sports car that filled her with automotive lust. His car would hug the road and curves... She refused to consider how hands that would caress the steering wheel would feel on her skin.

He was driving her crazy—as he had years ago, at least until homecoming. They'd first met because he'd been her brother's teammate. Then he'd been a beacon of friendship in her first accelerated math class, when the school decided anyone with her math ability needed to be advanced.

She climbed into her Tahoe and exhaled a frustrated sigh.

Twenty minutes later, after driving the speed limit and watching for the deer that tended to run across rural roads this time of year, Sierra joined Jack at Miller's Grill. Owned and operated by the descendants of the first Miller who'd settled in the area over two hundred years ago, the rustic-themed venue served great food in a casual, historic Western-saloon-style atmosphere. This late on a Sunday, Sierra didn't feel out of place in her T-shirt and jeans. However, she had thrown on a long-sleeve, crew neck sweater, which she always kept in the back seat in case of fall chill. Mrs. Miller showed them to a two-top in a quiet corner of the main dining room. Although she already knew what she'd order, Sierra studied her menu to avoid being caught studying Jack, who seemed to have trouble deciding.

Jack set his menu down. "I've been here six times in the past few weeks and never know what to get, it's all so good." He gazed around. "This place never changes. Looks the same as it did when we were kids."

He'd initiated small talk, the kind designed to break the awkward silence caused by menu reading. Not wanting to feel as if she was on a date, she chose to engage. "One thing I like about Beaumont is that certain things are always reliable in a world full of uncertainty."

One corner of his full lips lifted. "Like cobblestones, cookies filled with love, delicious wine and your hating me?"

And once he repeated her words, she winced. She'd come off sounding petty and harsh. "I was joking. Maybe strong dislike is better? I have good reasons."

A laugh she'd already come to like and appreciate accompanied an easy smile that sent the bouncy balls skittering. "That's fair," he conceded. "I am trying to buy your parents' business. It's always emotional when trying to put a dollar value on something built with a lot of blood, sweat, love, effort and tears."

Should she be suspicious he'd agreed with her? "Exactly. And you haven't yet convinced me you're honorable in your intentions toward them."

Had he been honorable to the other owners he'd bought out? Beaumont's wine country had been a tight-knit community and while her mom knew all the comings and goings, she'd been occupied with Sierra's dad's treatments. She hadn't mentioned anything to her daughter.

A nameless, faceless corporation taking over bothered Sierra a great deal. What would happen to the personal touches the region was known for?

"I'll show you around tomorrow. Tonight is about convincing you not to hate—dislike me," he amended. "The way to a man's heart is through his stomach. What's the way to a woman's? Are you the flowers-and-chocolate type?"

She scoffed. "No." She deliberately held his greenish-blue gaze, the one that she'd drown in if not careful. She was already feeling over her head as they'd fallen back into the easy banter they'd had during their tutoring sessions. "You could give me your car. That might be a start. I'd definitely like that."

He laughed, but not at her expense. "It is a beauty, isn't it? If I didn't think you'd drive her like a fighter pilot and try to reach supersonic speed, I might let you take the wheel."

"What, you think I drive like a bat out of hell and won't ride with me? I wouldn't have thought you a chicken."

"Nope. More like older and wiser," he countered. "Do you remember the tractor races at the county fair? You always won. If you drive cars or fly jets like you drove that tractor, you'd scare the crap out of me. I've never seen a tractor move that fast."

She fingered the handle of her fork. "That was a wild night. I still have that trophy somewhere."

He tilted his head slightly and studied her. "You scarred me for life. If I see a tractor, I quake in my shoes. You lapped all of us."

"Please," Sierra deadpanned. "You're fine. My dad likes to tinker on engines and, well, we might have overshot the modifications and souped my engine too much. It was quite the ride, though. I like it superfast."

"I bet you do. Although there's something to be said for nice and slow too."

He wasn't talking about tractors anymore, and Sierra took a long cold drink. Jack was as easy to be with as ever, and she had to remember that this wasn't a real date. She was here for food and information, and not necessarily in that order. "That's why my family lent you a dud." He'd come in dead last.

"We were more city people. I love my parents, but tractor people they were not."

That was true. Jack's family had lived in a 1980s development of oversize homes on five to ten acres just west of Beaumont proper. Her family had an expanded farmhouse. His had had a mansion built to look like something found in one of the turn-of-the-century, old-money St. Louis neighborhoods near Forest Park.

They were already opposites. When she'd found out about the bet, she'd felt so inferior. All her starry-eyed dreams had been nothing but castles in the air. Now she had to remember she was older, wiser, and a warrior.

"Do you know what you want?" Jack asked.

Miller's was famous for its burnt ends. Legend said Kurt Miller had learned directly from African American Henry Penny, who'd owned the first barbecue restaurant in the 1920s. Penny had inspired other greats such as Jack Stack and Arthur Bryant, who'd put the Kansas City region on the map. Food was easy to choose. But when it came to Jack, she had no idea what she wanted.

"Do you want anything else to drink besides water?"

She shook her head and let more cold water soothe her parched throat. "I've had a long day. I'll sugar up if we leave room for dessert. If we make it that far."

"Ye of little faith. Dessert gives me a goal to work toward. We'll stick with water," Jack told their server. "And we're ready."

After taking their order, their server returned with a basket containing Miller's famous homemade brown oat bread and whipped honey butter. Sierra reached for one of the slices and bit into the soft, delicious bread, enjoying how the hint of espresso and chocolate mixed with the flavor of the honey butter. "This stuff is so good."

"Nothing quite like it, huh? It was something I missed when I moved. Among other things."

She nibbled another bite and thought about, and dismissed, asking Jack about the bet. If her family's winery was going to be in competition with his, best not ruin the night before getting the information he'd promised. "Is this the part of the night where we share all our past secrets and foibles?"

He gave a small shrug. "I don't know. You tell me."

She shook her forefinger at him. "Oh, no, no. You invited me, and you're the guy who always had an answer for everything, so you don't get off that easily. This isn't a date, so what do two people talk about on a nondate?"

Another shrug. "No clue. This is new territory for me. You said it's not a business meeting."

"No, you said that and I agreed," she countered. "New territory or not, don't say the weather or people we both might know."

Jack winced. "That leaves politics, never a safe subject. The food here, which we've covered. There's your time in the navy."

"Classified."

He paused, his gaze assessing her. "Okay, off-limits. Since I'm trying not to antagonize you, on we go. What about hobbies? I like to hike, especially when I'm on vacation, which I force myself to take or I'd work nonstop. Are hobbies and travel safe topics for a nondate?"

"Hiking works. While Missouri may not have huge mountains, there are tons of trails besides the Katy. What about mountain biking? I like that."

"Nah, not into mountain biking. I did climb a bunch of peaks in Rocky Mountain National Park two summers ago." He unwrapped his black cloth napkin and set it in his lap. "Maybe we can hike together sometime."

That would be a date. Sierra sidestepped the question. "Well, we got through the hobby topic fast. I guess we're on to travel."

"I'm always traveling, actually. Mostly for business, which means every moment is booked. It's getting to actually stop and see the places that's been my problem. Normally I'm go, go, go from the moment I reach my destination. Today was a chance to stop, sit and drink some wine and now have some dinner. That's rare."

"I'm sure you talked business over wine today."

"Guilty for that earlier. Not now. What about you? Surely you saw the world."

"Sadly no. My entire naval career was mostly Stateside. My time on a carrier was spent going from San Diego to Pearl Harbor-Hickam before the carrier readied for a longer deployment. Then before it left Hawaii, I was sent to Pensacola."

"You hopefully saw a little of the islands."

"I did some island hopping when I was on leave, but I'm sure the average tourist has done much more. Hawaii's beautiful. I'd love to take a cruise." Then again, unless she climbed onto a plane, she couldn't even get to the ship's dock.

"We've got several small resorts on Oahu so I've been there a lot. Would you go back, maybe spend more time there when you aren't rushed?"

She thought for a minute, remembering her impressions from five years ago. "Maybe. The Pacific is so different from the Atlantic, and even the Gulf. To the average person, they might all be salty ocean water, but there's temperature differential, tides and then the color and size of the sand, and even air currents. There's something about the white sand beaches of the Gulf. Hawaii, as you know, is all volcanic and doesn't have the source of quartz Florida does. The white sand comes from the carbonate shells of marine organisms that have broken down." Seeing his arched eyebrow, she added self-consciously, "I'm a bit of a nerd about these things."

"I didn't know that about the sand. I'm finding your knowledge impressive, not nerdy."

"I majored in aerospace engineering. I always was the math geek, as you know."

"I wouldn't say you're a geek either. Brainy, maybe. Much smarter than me when it comes to numbers. And personally I think girls who know math and science are attractive."

She couldn't acknowledge that compliment, or how it made tingles begin. "Not at Beaumont High. The Pythagorean theorem and Newton's laws? The theory of relativity? Mention those in public and people's eyes glaze over. It's like in the movie *Mean Girls*. Mathletes like me were social outcasts. Anyway, thankfully, there's been a real push this past decade for women to not only go into STEM fields but to excel. Heck, we wouldn't have gotten to the moon without Katherine Johnson. Her fight to be at the forefront and to be respected was twice as hard because she was a woman of color."

Their server interrupted then, coming over to refill their water glasses and tell them their food would be right out.

Sierra moved her spoon an inch or two from side

to side, sliding it along the table. "Sorry, I get rather passionate about gender equity and respect. I was a flight instructor, and a female one at that."

Which made her crash doubly hard. Would a man have been as scrutinized as she'd been? She knew the logical answer was yes, but doubt still lingered. Women had to work twice as hard to achieve what a man did with less effort, and women absorbed triple the guilt along the way. "Anyway, moving on to something more cheery please."

"Don't change topics on my account," Jack said. "I like finding out what makes you tick."

Yes, but she'd not intended to share something personal. Already her body wished this was a date. But the last thing she needed at this critical juncture of her life was to become entangled with Jack. "Don't look too hard. You may not like what you see."

"So far I'm liking what I see. Very much." He gave her a reassuring smile that seemed more serious in its purpose than it was flirty. "You're a fascinating woman, Sierra James. A man would have to be out of his mind not to see that and be attracted to you."

She managed not to blush as his words landed on her with the impact he'd intended. Damn, he was good. If she didn't watch herself, she'd fall for Jack all over again, as she had when she'd been young and naive. Almost a decade and a half later,

she should be older, wiser and far less foolish. She
should be oblivious to his charms. However, try telling that to her heart, which beat faster whenever he
was around. They'd always had this strange wave-
length, and it had reignited as if he'd never wounded
her to her core all those years before.

He offered a smile she feared to trust and take at
face value. Her heart had made that mistake once,
with devastating results. Now it wasn't her virginity on the line but her parents' winery. "Yeah, well,"
she managed, keeping her reaction to his compliment vague.

Besides, what could she say? No way would she
tell him that he wasn't too shabby on the eyes either. He was like a down-to-earth movie star who,
despite his attractiveness, remained the quintessen-
tial boy next door. Despite herself, she was enjoying his company. She found him witty, intriguing
and funny. His politeness and charm came pack-
aged with good looks, impeccable manners and the
ability to make conversation. He was a triple threat,
somehow making her believe that maybe he wasn't
as bad as her memories said he was, as if she'd made
a mistake thinking him a jerk. But all of that was
on the surface. Who was he, really? The boy who'd
tricked her years earlier...or someone else entirely?

He watched her thoughtfully, his lowered lashes
and smoldering eyes communicating evident interest. What would it be like to stroke the side of his

face and learn the texture? Would his kiss knock her socks off? In high school, he'd set the highest standard with one kiss. That momentous feeling, the desire and press of his lips on hers, remained etched into her memory as one of the best moments of her life. Then discovering the bet had brought the residual high crashing down and shattered her faith.

She was an adult now who'd worked hard to reach her dreams, only to be knocked literally out of the air. She had priorities other than entering a relationship and having sex. Even if she had the impression she and Jack would ignite the sheets should they ever get together, their chemistry was that tangible, the last thing she needed was another life letdown, especially one she entered like a moth beating against a dusk-to-dawn light.

"Sierra?" he prompted. "What are you thinking?"

Nervous he could read her innermost thoughts, Sierra glanced over his shoulder. Their server approached, two plates in hand. She indicated his arrival. "Food's here."

Saved by the brisket.

Chapter Seven

For being a nondate, things had certainly heated ten-plus degrees. After their server set down their brisket and sides, Jack used the opportunity to steer the conversation into safer waters but delving into topics beyond "how's your food?" Answer—delicious.

Sierra proved to be a fantastic conversationalist and he enjoyed listening to her. They discussed music, sports and cars. In music, she liked alternative, such as Bastille, Muse and Joywave. He was into classic rock, such as U2 and the Rolling Stones, whom he'd seen on their last world tour. They both liked hockey and baseball, but found themselves at odds over their favorite sports teams. He'd adopted San Jose's hockey team and San Francisco's professional baseball team. Her loyalties had remained firmly in St. Louis, even when she'd lived elsewhere. When they'd talked cars, they'd found common ground. They both loved sleek machines and high speed. She held more knowledge about classic cars in her pinkie than some of his car collector friends who owned the vehicles they discussed.

"They just like saying they have a certain model. It's not like they're ever going to reach a Jay Leno level of collecting," he told Sierra, mentioning the former *Tonight Show* talk show host. "He's got like, what? One hundred and eighty-one cars? That's not even including all his motorcycles."

"Yeah, he's beyond museum grade," Sierra agreed. "He's his own museum."

"More power to him. I can understand the appeal, but it's not me. I'm not that passionate about cars. They get you from point A to B."

"Yet you drive a current-year Mercedes convertible," she pointed out.

"Touché. I do like getting there in style."

"What about your house? Huge, I bet."

"You'd be wrong." He saw her eyebrows lift in surprise. "I own a two-bedroom condo. A thousand square feet. I'm not there enough to enjoy it." He fingered his water glass. "Eventually stuff is simply stuff."

They ate in silence for a moment until Sierra filled the gap. "Do you remember Bruce? He had that Triumph Spitfire? I coveted that car. They're not worth much these days, not like the vehicles that go for small fortunes at Barrett-Jackson auctions."

"I went to one of those with one of my friends. It was crazy. Remember my old Pontiac Grand Prix? My dad constantly warned me not to wreck it. I was so afraid I'd hit a deer or something."

Sierra shrugged. "You had a car. I shared with Zoe the same Ford Focus my older brothers drove. The only reason it made it as long as it did after everyone battered it is because my dad worked on cars. But what you drive now is classy and hits zero to sixty in about six-point-one seconds." She set down her fork. "Letting you drive tomorrow at least has the benefit I'll get to ride in it. Especially if it has all the bells and whistles."

"I bought it fully loaded." He didn't add he'd bought it sight unseen a few months ago, after he'd arrived in Missouri with suitcases in hand. Instead Jack grinned at her, liking when she reciprocated. Smiling changed her face, making her appear much less serious and far more approachable. Even back in elementary school, she'd had this studied, pensive look. Her brows would knit together as she solved a math problem. Her gaze would lock onto something with laser focus, those thoughtful brown eyes moving side to side as she took everything in.

Many saw the academically accelerated Sierra rightfully as smarter than them, and wrongfully they reacted badly. Because of this, Sierra had carried a slight chip on her shoulder. She'd been an interloper. She was the "smarty-pants" who'd advanced two grades in math and been placed into a class of mostly unenlightened boys who'd resented that a girl could solve equations faster than they could. The disparity grew in middle school and high school—where the focus for many girls was on popularity. Sierra had been more interested in playing chess and learning to fly than worrying about the latest fashion trends. She'd get her hands dirty modifying a tractor with her dad while some of her peers were more concerned about chipping their nails.

Sierra's focus never wavered—she'd fixated on soaring far beyond Beaumont, both literally and figuratively. She'd always held her own against the teenage flow of dumb ideas, which he'd admired, even if he'd been too immature to respond appropriately when his friends had teased him about her. Or when they'd made comments directly to her face. In hindsight, he should have told them to stop. Not that she'd ever needed rescuing. But he could have been more cognizant of his playing into his high school's old-fashioned and irrelevant stereotypes. He'd found her both interesting and attractive. He still did.

He could tell her all this, but bringing up the past probably wasn't a wise move, not at this exact moment when they'd actually managed to get through dinner with more than a semblance of détente. She'd shot him down in high school. Turned him down flat with a "I'm not here for your entertainment," which even he knew had come from one of Pink's pop songs. One message delivered loud and clear.

Their server removed their plates, forming a natural break.

"Do you still want dessert?" Jack asked, not ready to end the evening. Maybe that made him a fool, but despite their past, he'd enjoyed getting to know the woman she'd become. "It's probably not as good as anything your mom bakes, but..."

"Is anything?" Sierra chuckled.

"No. Your mom makes a fantastic cookie. Now you're making them."

"For now. I finally have the how-to-cook part sort of figured out. Even though I baked nonstop in my mom's kitchen, baking in the store creates its own kind of stress. There's a standard. A pressure to perform."

"I understand. My parents' livelihood rests on my shoulders. This project? If I can't deliver, I let them down and all our employees down. It's a lot to live up to." He'd never admitted that to anyone. Thankfully she didn't judge him.

"Well, I did fail. My first few batches were terrible and inedible. I couldn't get the recipe right no matter how hard I tried. My mom was patient. In fact, I'd done great work until you appeared. You made me burn an entire batch."

"Me?" Incredulous, he pointed to his chest. "What did I do?"

"You made me so distracted, I missed the timer going off. We do not serve overdone cookies in our shop."

"Wasn't my intention to ruin cookies." He grinned. "Good to know I can distract you, though."

She wagged a finger at him. "Not sure that's a good thing, so don't let it go to your head. It's big enough."

It pleased him she wasn't indifferent. Maybe they could put the past behind them and find some sort of new ground. "That's right. You dislike me."

"You haven't been too terrible to be around tonight." She gestured, as if waving off that thread of conversation. "I'd be happy to split a crème brûlée. My mom hates making custard, so since even the great Jayne James has to have at least one culinary weakness, it's not something I eat often. And when we come here, it's always the mantra of 'you know there's dessert at home' so we leave after the entrées."

He wanted to please her. "Crème brûlée it is. Are you sure you don't want your own?"

She pointed to her clean plate. "I'm stuffed from dinner and it's too filling. A few bites will suffice."

"Perfect. We'll split it. A crème brûlée with two spoons," he told the server, who'd materialized. Once he'd gone, Jack studied Sierra. She'd relaxed as the night went on. "Our dessert sounds much better than serving you the standard fare of cookies."

"Even if I truly hated you, Auntie Jayne's would never serve you burned cookies."

"That's good because once the hotel gets built, I'd like to serve Auntie Jayne's cookies. Whether or not I buy your winery, that's one of my goals. We serve the best in our hotels, and we try to keep as many products as possible local. We are good neighbors."

Sierra nibbled a lower lip he longed to taste. "You'd have to talk to my mom and sister about that."

"I plan on it. But now we're discussing business, which we said was a no-go zone. It's my fault as I'm the one who said no shop talk. Deliberately changing subjects, if you could have any one car, what would it be?"

"You mean besides the ones sitting in my dad's garage? A Porsche 911. Doesn't matter what year or what color. If I ever ride in one, I hope it lives up to the hype."

"It's a Porsche. It will."

Their server returned carrying a white ramekin. Jack pointed. "You get the first bite."

Her spoon cracked through the top brown crystallized layer with a satisfying crunch, revealing the golden custard beneath. She closed her lips around the bite and Jack checked a groan. Her eyes involuntarily closed for a second as she savored the delicious flavor hitting her tongue. She withdrew the spoon with a little pop and stared at him.

"That good, huh?" he asked, amusement in his ragged tone.

Her cheeks flushed. "That good."

Boldly she dug her spoon into the custard. Unlike most of the women he knew, Sierra gave him no cutesy embarrassed gesture bordering on flirtation. Instead she waved her spoon like a flag before scooping a third bite. "I've changed my mind. You should get your own."

"No, you don't." He stretched forward and stuck his spoon into the ramekin before she could slide it to her side of the table. "We're sharing."

"If you insist." Sierra sucked in another morsel. "It's delicious."

Jack shifted, the front of his pants suddenly tight. "I'm glad I did something to lessen your dislike of me."

"Don't get all cocky, or you'll ruin the moment," she warned. However, he noted the hints of mirth in the way fine lines crinkled around her luminous brown eyes.

He scooped more custard, working from the edge of the ramekin closest to him toward the middle until only a few bites remained. He set his spoon down, leaned back and placed his hands on his stomach. "Last few are yours."

Sierra dug her spoon in. "You don't have to tell

me twice. Look at us getting along. Must be the good food."

He hoped they'd get along beyond the food. He opened his mouth to tell her that, but before he could speak, he heard a deep male voice boom, "Jack Clayton? Is that you? It is you. And with Sierra James. Fancy seeing you both together."

Crap. "Hey, Randy. Paula." Jack acknowledged the last two people he wanted to see right now, two of his former classmates, had Jack stayed at Beaumont High. Randy had assumed ownership of his father's grocery store chain. He sported thinning hair he tried to comb over and carried the pounds of a middle-aged man whose exercise consisted of driving a golf cart around eighteen holes. Jack took some petty satisfaction in knowing he hadn't let his body go. While Jack and Randy might have run in the same crowd, they'd not been close friends.

"Heard you were back in town," Randy boomed. "Surprised we hadn't run into you before now."

"Been dealing more with the county council than the chamber," Jack said. A purposeful move. "An oversight I plan to rectify." A small white lie.

"We should get together. Maybe make it a foursome for golf, if Paula's not busy. We have kids in middle school, and Paula chairs all sorts of committees."

The former homecoming queen smiled. Still paper-thin, she wore a bright floral skirt, a silk shirt and a curious expression.

Across the table, Jack could see Sierra bristling with…hatred? Animosity? Time to leave before the great evening turned unsalvageable, especially as Randy tended to come across like a bull charging the streets of Pamplona, a characteristic made worse by his position on the chamber's executive board. The man was a menace who was ruining Jack's evening with Sierra.

"Didn't take you two long to reconnect," Randy said.

Jack held back a growl as Randy proved that while he might have business acumen, he lacked tact, same as in high school when he'd commanded the social scene.

But before Jack could diffuse the situation Randy remained oblivious to creating, Sierra rested her chin on her thumbs. She gazed at Randy with an indecipherable expression that gave Jack pause. "Do you have a problem with that?" Her tone held no emotion. No warning. Which made her even deadlier. She must have been formidable in the cockpit.

Randy's face reddened. "No, no. Of course not." He flubbed for an answer. "Paula and I saw you and wanted to be friendly."

Sierra didn't even blink. "Actually, you wanted to discover what you could wrangle out of Jack, both personally and professionally, especially since he's buying all the properties on Winery Road."

Damn. Jack was impressed. The navy had turned Sierra into a straight shooter who hit the bull's-eye dead on.

Paula, who clearly had better social navigation skills, especially when a situation wasn't going her husband's way, gave a pert laugh designed to diffuse the tension. She brushed a strand of hair behind her ear, revealing a tiny diamond stud. "Actually, we do have an ulterior motive, but it's mine, not Randy's. We need two more people to help organize the town's Halloween festival. Your mom always participates, Sierra, but she's stepped down and I haven't found her replacement. Could you fill in? I'm surprised she hadn't asked you to take her place."

Before Sierra could reject the offer, Paula turned to Jack. "You could help Sierra."

"I sent you a check," he told her. "Should be there by Tuesday."

"Which we're grateful for. But I need hands-on help. Both of you would be perfect," Paula pressed. "Especially as the two of you are a couple?"

Damn it. There it was. She'd dropped that bait so expertly. How to extract both him and Sierra from this increasingly awkward and tense situation? "Really, Paula, we haven't synced our schedules. We both work and I've got several important projects in the queue. We can't commit. I'm sorry."

Sierra's expression turned artificially sweet, causing Jack immediate worry. She reached her hand across the table to pat his hand. "Jack, surely you can make the time to prove how good of a community supporter you're going to be? What's that saying about good neighbors?"

Jack's eyes narrowed. The minx was enjoying his discomfort. Well, two could play this game. "Sierra, didn't you also tell me about wanting to become more involved with the town, especially now that you're living here again?"

Paula gave a delighted squeal and clapped her hands. "Oh, I'm so glad we can count on your both."

"Jack is the one you really want," Sierra said quickly. "He's much more business oriented than I am." If looks could kill, Jack would be a dead man.

Still alive, he nipped her escape in the bud. No way would she wedge him into working with these two. "Sierra and I are meeting tomorrow at eleven. Email me the details, say by ten, so Sierra and I can review them. If we can help, we will. But we reserve the right to bow out gracefully. Sierra and I are very busy."

"Look at you, all formal," Randy harrumphed, clearly displeased with not being the center of attention. "It won't be anything you can't handle. It'll be like old times."

Jack had no desire for old times. Sierra's expression soured and she glared at Randy, her ire evident.

Her next words came out sounding light and airy, yet they were delivered with bitter sarcasm that lay on an underlying bed of steel. "What, you're going to place bets on whether Jack and I do the deed? Homecoming was a five-dollar buy-in. What's it worth now? Five hundred? A thousand? You know, with inflation and all."

What the actual hell? Jack's gaze ping-ponged from Randy, who blinked and sputtered, to Sierra, who folded her arms across her chest and sat there like a stoic Cheshire cat. Paula studied something on the dark paneling across the room.

Something was afoot. What was this about a bet? Was this why Sierra hated him all these years? What had Randy done? Where was their missing server? While Jack tried to extricate them from the situation, Sierra set her napkin on the table.

"Paula, send Jack an email tomorrow morning. Jack, give Paula your card. Paula, we'll be in touch."

"Thank you. I'll do that."

Randy appeared as if he was going to add more, but between Paula placing her hand on his arm and Jack's glare, he wisely instead said, "Great to see you both. We'll catch up soon," and followed his wife toward the entrance.

Sierra waited until they were out of sight before pushing her chair back. An angry aura simmered and her words came out frosty. "Thank you for an enlightening evening. I'm leaving now."

It was as if a pendulum had swung the other direction and he'd entered a different reality from their earlier camaraderie, one completely dark and lifeless. "You first going to tell me what that was all about?"

She stared at him. "Which part? The part where we're a couple or the one where he has no memories of placing bets on my virginity? That was why you asked me to homecoming, wasn't it? Because everyone knew you wanted to ask Laurel Lovelace, who was prettier, had bigger boobs and put out. But Randy dangled my virginity as a carrot you couldn't resist."

"I asked you because I wanted to go with you." The truth was too little, too late and fell short of the mark. Jack's mind worked frantically to put together the pieces of a situation he didn't yet fully understand.

Disappointed, Sierra gave a vigorous shake of her head, her short hair barely moving. "Lies don't become you. I was never in your league. A lowly freshman nerd. A mathlete. You were junior class homecoming rep, which I'm sure ticked Randy off. I was a joke to you all. Please—" she drew out the word with derision "—don't insult me by pretending otherwise about your motives for asking me out."

She was on her feet and Jack stared at her. "I'm missing something."

"My life wasn't some teen-movie plot you and

your friends could try on for fun and laughs." The chair shoved in with a thunk that shook the table. "Since I do want to see your plan for this town and why you want my parents' winery so badly, I'll expect you at eleven. One minute late and the whole thing is off."

Before he could say another word, she was gone. Damn it. Finally catching their server's attention, Jack paid the bill. By the time he'd finished, he knew Sierra would be halfway home.

Tonight they'd laughed and enjoyed themselves. Then Randy had to come over and ruin it. At least Jack had a better idea why Sierra hated him. Sixteen years ago, he'd been guilty by association, an unwilling accomplice to what his so-called friends had done—apparently some sort of bet about homecoming, a bet he'd never known about. As a man who prided himself on his integrity, the weight was on his shoulders to find out the whole story, make amends and fix it. A bet to take her virginity? That was unconscionable. He'd thought he was asking out, to a dance, a girl he'd crushed on forever. He'd known he was moving, but he'd wanted one date with the one who'd been a constant in his life since she'd been a precocious kindergartener sitting in many of his second-grade classes. Her virginity had not been his goal, even if that one time he'd kissed her had blown his mind and he'd hoped and prayed he'd get to kiss her again.

Had the popular kids really been so cruel? Jack didn't doubt it. Randy had always been a pompous asshole too full of himself—he still was. But Jack hadn't known about any bet involving Sierra. Clearly she thought he was in on it and had rejected him.

Now he was trying to buy her family's winery. Tonight he'd thought he was cracking her shell and penetrating her armor. Instead, she'd outflanked him and left him dying on the grass. What did he do next? He liked Sierra. Fate had brought them back together and he wanted to get to know her. Yet at the same time, he couldn't fail to deliver Jamestown to his parents, and no way in hell did Sierra want to sell.

Crap. Crap. Crap.

Chapter Eight

Sierra had been awake for hours. She'd gone for a five-mile run. She'd met her best friend, Emily, at Clara's Café, a place with ancient wooden tables and chairs, kitschy decor and lard in every fluffy, made-from-scratch pastry. Saying the hell with counting calories and carbs, Sierra had ordered a cinnamon roll.

Taking comfort in the mix of cinnamon swirl and cream cheese frosting, she'd confessed what had happened the night before, her recap taking the same length of time it had taken for Emily to seep her turmeric and ginger tea. Emily had listened without commenting until she removed the tea bag and set it on a small china plate. "You had quite the night."

Quite the understatement, but Emily hadn't been done. She'd offered tons of suggestions, as she tended to do. Sierra mulled over some of them as she glanced at the bedside clock. She prepped for Jack's arrival, exchanging her breakfast attire of joggers and an oversize crew neck sweatshirt from her Academy days for a red short-sleeve shirt with matching buttons, blue jeans and distressed white sneakers. She brushed her short hair and added a swipe of clear lip gloss. There. She didn't look like something the cat dragged in or someone who'd slept fitfully, worrying she might have torpedoed herself last night by walking out. While verbally smacking Randy down had felt great, revealing her emotions offered Jack weaponry. She didn't want to put herself into a position where she couldn't win. She did not want to crash and burn. She also wanted to protect her family. That's what worried her most—how would they handle the loss of the vineyard should competition from Jack's vineyards force them out? Her dad's past was clear as a bell. His present was hazy and fading in and out.

Sierra would love for her dad to know her children, but unless she followed through and visited that fertility specialist friend of Emily's, the probability was higher that Sierra would climb into a cockpit and fly at a supersonic speed before she met a man, married him and birthed a brood.

Sierra moved to the porch. At two minutes to

eleven, Sierra watched as the convertible slowly covered the gravel drive. She calmed shot nerves. "Look at you," she quipped as he stepped out. Damn, but he looked good in blue jeans that complimented every inch, a forest green Henley and boat shoes sans socks. "Right on time."

He pushed his sunglasses atop his head. "I took you seriously. After last night, I wasn't sure you weren't going to back out of this and text me you were canceling."

She lifted a small cross-body purse strap over her shoulder. "I considered it. But I want to know what you're doing with the wineries, especially as it affects my family."

"Then let's go. I have no secrets and am on the up-and-up. Speaking of, are we going to talk about last night? Because I'd like to figure out what happened and say I'm sorry for whatever I did. I thought we were having a great time until Randy and Paula interrupted us. What happened back in high school? Clearly I missed something."

His earnest expression made Sierra eye him skeptically. They had been having fun until Randy arrived. She'd been amazed how well she and Jack had gotten along. He'd made her laugh. Once he'd been a nemesis, the man who'd asked her out with the goal of humiliating her. He was Jerk Clayton. But dinner had allowed Sierra a glimpse of a Jack she could fall for, until reality rushed in like a party crasher. While he'd appeared shocked when she'd brought up the bet about her virginity, she hadn't been able to read Jack's reaction. Maybe he'd been surprised she'd known about it? Maybe he hadn't known, after all? Could she trust him to tell her the truth all these years later?

Thinking about the entire situation made her blood pressure rise, and if she and Jack talked about high school today, most likely they'd get into an argument, she'd storm inside and then she'd never know what he had planned for Beaumont, or why he wanted her family's winery. She would protect her family's businesses, which meant being pleasant and getting in his car.

She would compartmentalize. She would be singularly focused. When she'd been in the air, her entire mind had been on flying. Not her bills. Not a conflict with one of her students. Not the fact she had to call apartment maintenance for her malfunctioning washing machine. She stayed on track, which she determined to do now.

"Last night was personal, and today is about business. How about we not mix the two this early and ruin things. I genuinely want to hear about your plans."

"I can respect that," Jack agreed. He glanced around, noting the landscape and the closed garage doors. "It's quiet. Peaceful."

Did he want to catch her dad? Perhaps have a

chat about buying the winery? She nipped that in the bud. "Everyone's gone. They won't be back until late."

Sierra rounded to the passenger side and sunk onto soft, buttery leather. As a car lover, she noted the dashboard's high-end features and the center console designed for the driver's pleasure. Jack clicked his seat belt. The engine turned over with a generous and satisfying purr.

The top down, he drove at a snail's pace along the gravel drive in order to avoid churning gray dust. Reaching the blacktop, he accelerated onto the state highway, the g-force pushing Sierra against the seat. Fall color lined Winery Road and a breeze ruffled through her hair and blew on her face. Sierra admittedly enjoyed the ride.

Jack pressed a button on the steering wheel, lowering the radio volume. "We'll stop at Elephant Rock first. One of the changes I'm making is to the specific branding of each winery. Jamestown, for instance, has a Yellowstone feel."

"More Yosemite," Sierra corrected. "It's modeled after the Tenyana Lodge's Grand Lobby, a place my mom and dad fell in love with while on vacation."

"Jamestown is a spectacular venue on par with those in California and Oregon. I also like how you serve wines that hail from Australia and New Zealand alongside your own."

"That was my dad's idea. We do a wine exchange

program with some of the wineries there. It allows our customers a chance to experience near and far, and as my dad puts it, it exposes people around the world to our products."

"I love it. I'm planning something similar. While each of our Beaumont wineries will still have its own branded wines, each will also stock other Clayton vintages. That way if you want a Norton from Elephant Rock and a Vignoles from Primrose Hill, that's possible. While the number of offerings will be limited, customers will be able to mix and match, even when purchasing a case. We may include some of Clayton's West Coast vintages. We haven't decided."

"If you can get it all in one stop, won't that defeat the point of visiting each winery?" she asked.

Jack expertly navigated a tight S-curve, the car hugging the pavement. "Our research showed that while some customers winery hop, most choose to return to their favorite place. They find one they like and it becomes their go-to winery where they spend the majority of their time and money. We're planning to cater to that. Think about how Disney sets up its parks and hotels. Each venue has its own distinctive personality. There's the Grand Floridian, or the Polynesian, or the Contemporar, which are all different but all on the monorail line. Even the parks have distinct personalities. That's my goal. The wineries around Beaumont are more or less the same, with the exception of Jamestown. But there's potential for so much more. I see Elephant Rock as an adventurous winery, a place where cyclists and hikers enjoying the Katy Trail can stop for a wood-fired pizza and a refreshing bottle of wine or mock-tails made with verjus."

His mention of verjus had Sierra realizing how completely Jack had thought through his plans. Verjus was juice made from unripened grapes. To allow the majority of grapes to ripen, vintners culled those clusters before veraison, or the stage where the grapes began to turn colors and develop sugars. This allowed the rest of the crop to mature.

But instead of tossing the immature grapes and letting them rot, verjus creators squeezed the under-developed grapes into a liquid that was then used as a vinegar substitute. Jamestown's chef used verjus to braise meat and as a flavor in his homemade salad dressings. Jerry, Jamestown's lead bartender, mixed verjus with sparkling water and strained it with fruits such as blueberries, blackberries, straw-berries or raspberries. When garnished with a mint or basil leaf, the result was a golden nonalcoholic cocktail that, when strained, had the same body as a Vignoles. Sierra's dad had begun to experiment with bottling verjus a few years ago, but he hadn't made the juice a major business focus. "Are you planning on exporting it?"

"Verjus is currently a hot commodity, so yes."

Jack put on his blinker as he turned into Elephant Rock. "We view verjus production as a growth area."

No wonder the area owners had sold their wineries. Clayton Holdings had the resources and vision to dominate the region. Already, Sierra could see the changes in Elephant Rock from the parking lot. A fresh coat of brown paint covered vertical boards while new white paint outlined all the window and door trim.

The vibe was north woods cabin, complete with an oversize stone firepit circled by alternating green and red Adirondack chairs. At the edge of the lawn, several visitors sunned themselves on the weathered remains of large boulders made of Precambrian granite. Rows of picnic tables stood in a small meadow open to the sky, while others sat under a small pavilion with a raised platform for musical acts. As if proving Jack's point, cyclists dressed in riding gear lounged at one of the tables, their bikes and helmets stored in a nearby rack as they ate personal-sized pizzas.

Sierra followed Jack to a large bar located inside a screened porch. In the winter, the space could be glassed in for year-round use. The entire vibe was of summer camp mess hall, but with more sophistication and built for adults.

"Mr. Clayton." A late thirties man who wore jeans and a light plaid shirt with the sleeves rolled up greeted them. "Did we have a meeting?"

Jack shook the man's outstretched hand. "Nope. I'm taking my friend Sierra on a tour. Sierra, this is Dan. I lured him down from Oregon. He has a degree in horticulture. Dan, do you have time to work us through a tasting? I know that's not your usual job, but Sierra's family owns Jamestown."

"Sure thing." Dan gave her a friendly smile. "You have a great Norton."

"We do," Sierra agreed.

Dan reached for two empty wineglasses. "I wasn't sure about this climate, but it's growing on me." He chuckled at his joke. "I've been developing a hybrid grape, and it'll grow better here."

"Dan's also enhancing some of our existing grapes, and tweaking the soil and such to make them taste better," Jack said.

"I love a challenge." Dan placed a glass in front of her. "We'll start with the white blend, which won a silver medal in the state fair two summers ago."

As Dan poured tasting samples, he explained the various grapes and flavor notes in a way similar to how Jamestown employees did. If the wine won an award, mention it. How many times had Sierra bragged about Jamestown's Norton? Too many to count.

Sierra inhaled the subtle aroma of peach and apple. She sipped. The wine was sweet, light and crisp. "That's good." Not as good as Jamestown's—what was?—but not shabby either.

"Excuse me a moment." Noticing something, Dan set down two tall glasses of water and went to speak with an employee.

Sierra studied the thin placard listing the wines available to taste. She held it out for Jack's inspection. "Weren't there more?"

"Good eye. We're curating and being selective in what we're serving at each location. Some wineries had ten vintages available, and that's too many when tastings are free, as most Beaumont winery tastings are. That's a lot of loss if it doesn't translate into sales."

"True. People go for the tastings and don't buy. They're after the buzz or killing an afternoon on the cheap."

"Why shouldn't they, if they can drink the equivalent of a free glass during a tasting at each place? Starting in March, we're instituting a five-dollar tasting fee at all our locations, good for five choices. We're following Jamestown's example."

"We apply the fee to any order of six or more bottles purchased at the end of tasting and taken to go. We don't apply it to bottles uncorked on-site."

"That's a good idea." Jack typed a note into his phone.

"Jamestown always sets the standard for this area," Sierra told him, pride evident.

"It does, which is one reason I like your business

model. Yours was the first place that didn't allow people to bring in their own food."

"My dad's contemporaries swore it would turn guests away, but having a full kitchen did the opposite. We drew bigger crowds."

A bittersweet pang faltered Sierra's joy. How many ideas remained trapped in her dad's brain, never to see the light of day? Damn the disease that daily robbed him.

Before her stress built, Dan returned and poured two more whites and two reds. The tasting diverted her from contemplating her family's problems, which included the attractive man to her left. His proximity gave her goose bumps. His mind bounced from idea to idea. None of Elephant Rock's wines impressed except the white blend, and that couldn't compare to what she served at Jamestown. But Sierra recognized the clientele choosing Elephant Rock wouldn't necessarily spend more for Jamestown's offerings, and they might feel underdressed in their cycling gear. Jamestown also didn't sport a game room with ping-pong, shuffleboard and a few classic pinball machines.

"Try this." Dan poured from a thin bottle.

"What do you think?" Jack asked.

Sierra tasted hints of blackberry in the deep red vintage. "Rustic, yet fun and decent. The tannins hit on the back. Very nice. As for Elephant Rock, it's clear you know your market and customer base."

Leaving Dan behind, she followed Jack over to the firepit, where lazy smoke floated toward a robin-egg sky. "I studied business at Stanford and followed that with an MBA. Did you always want to fly?"

"As much as Zoe wanted to bake. I'm fascinated by how things work, the engineering. I love studying thrust. Drag. Weight. Lift. The things it takes to put something in the air and keep it there. Not that there isn't math involved in making wine. Math is everywhere. But how long it takes grapes to grow, or what the soil condition must be, isn't really what excites me."

"Flying does."

"Yes." Even though she was now deathly afraid of climbing into the cockpit. Not that he needed to know that.

She and Jack wandered closer to the vineyard's namesake large rocks. A couple wearing bike shorts and Lycra shirts lounged on their backs, enjoying the sun. She turned her face heavenward, feeling the warmth for a moment. "What's next?"

"We head down the road to Primrose Hill, where we'll eat lunch. I heard your stomach grumbling."

"Isn't Primrose simply grab-and-go out of a cooler?"

Jack smiled. "Not anymore. But if you want a personal pizza, we can take one to go. Or you can wait a few more minutes."

She ignored the rumbling of her stomach that the offer of wood-fired pepperoni caused. "I can wait."

Five minutes later, the car ascended a winding, tree-lined driveway. Boasting the highest elevation, Primrose Hill's tasting room had once existed beneath a canopy of trees, as the vineyard's vines were located on another portion of the property. However, the farther the convertible climbed, the more the trees thinned, until at the top, instead of entering a dense woodland with a winery building in the center, half of the summit was now a meadow open to the sky and views of the floodplain.

Jack parked, and Sierra climbed out. A newly constructed stone wall ran around two sides of the property, separating grassy areas from the hillside. The changes provided a fabulous view of the Missouri River. "Wow."

"Thanks. We realized if we took out some of the trees—and don't worry, they went to good use and we did carbon offsets and planted others elsewhere—then we could create an experience of being at the top of the mountain without being on a mountain. We chose a chalet theme, which you can see in our choice of using a darker wood for the trim and shutters. We expect this to be a popular wedding destination. Construction starts in a week on an overlook deck."

"People will come just for the view." One Jamestown would never have. From this elevation, she could see the bend in the river and the bluffs of the next county over. Sierra followed Jack up the walkway's gentle incline in order to reach the tasting room.

Inside, what had been a utilitarian space gleamed with sparkly improvements that made midcentury modern and Frank Lloyd Wright meet Swiss Alps. Modern decor complemented wooden accent walls and high wood ceilings. "You have a great designer."

"Thanks. He suggested we film the renovations. We're hoping to get it on a channel like HGTV for the national exposure. We've also had local coverage."

Sierra considered the ramifications. People would flock to the area, providing the influx Jack wanted. The area would lose its sleepy vibe, but the trade-off was increased profit for area businesses, which in turn would provide jobs. Even Sierra could see the positives and how successful Jack's vision would be.

She wasn't surprised. Jack had always been able to turn his ideas into reality. Even as far back as elementary school, he'd been a natural leader, a pied piper with the plan. He'd learned people were his greatest resource, such as getting Sierra's help with his math homework. As much as she'd wanted to back out after last night's fiasco, she'd been smart to come. The tour had been eye-opening. Jack's plan would revolutionize the region. Her mom and dad had enough on their plate with her dad's illness. Soon they'd have to worry about increased competition and staying afloat.

Instead of the former sparse grab-and-go, Primrose Hill's glass sparkly display cases contained gourmet sandwiches ranging from chicken salad on croissant to roast beef on twist buns covered with poppy seeds. Several cases featured a variety of specialty baked breads, specialty cheeses and spreads, along with Swiss chocolates and personal-sized apple strudels.

"We upgraded Primrose's food by contracting with Vitale's Deli, figuring why not bring some of Main Street here? As much as possible, we want to partner with Main Street businesses. Like I said, I want Auntie Jayne's cookies in my hotel."

Which meant at least one of her family's businesses might survive. Not much of a concession.

Jack caught a clerk's attention, and she pivoted through a swinging door, returning with a large wicker picnic basket. Carrying their lunch, Jack led Sierra to a lovely gazebo that overlooked the flood plain and Missouri River beyond. He placed the basket on a four-top table marked Reserved. He removed melamine plates, thick paper napkins, stemless wineglasses and a bottle of a California red.

He uncorked the bottle. "Primrose is the place with all the views, but it's also the one with the worst-tasting wine. We've cut the offerings from the original ten to two Primrose vintages that meet our standards. As such, we're making this the place where Clayton's West Coast wines will be served, along with some of our other local wines." He gave a sweep of his arm. "Visitors come to Primrose for the view. Sort of how you'd go to Disney's Hollywood Studios for motion-picture-related fun and Disney World for princess castles, Primrose is about location. We wanted to keep the food perfect for picnic-style dining, allowing the kitchen to be used for catering weddings and receptions. As soon as the winery closes, it's ready for private events."

He poured a glass. "This is our Lodi Zinfandel. It was the wine that launched my dad's love for winemaking and, well, this quest. He was out in San Francisco and loved the wine so much that he bought a winery."

Made from a black-skinned grape, the Zinfandel was a robust dark red containing hints of fruits and round and soft tannins. Sierra swirled the glass, inhaled the aroma and wrapped her lips around the edge. "Very nice."

She indulged in another sip. She knew about Lodi, which was about seventy miles east of the San Francisco Bay. Known for its old vines, with some over one hundred years old, even without reading the label, she would have had no doubt this was one of those. "Cranberries and strawberries with a hint of spice. Oak barrels. Nice acidity and texture, and while dry, not disturbingly so. Finishes smooth."

Just like Jack. Charming yet disturbing in a "get under your skin" kind of way. He'd arranged the table while she sampled, and as he did, he passed over a cold bottle of water. In order not to block the view, he sat to her left. She was highly aware of him, and when he accidentally brushed her arm, shivers traveled up and down her spine.

He sipped from his glass. "Thank you for agreeing to go with me today. To good wine." He raised his glass, and Sierra clinked her glass to his. "This is probably my favorite out of everything we bottle," he said. "It's been great showing you what we do. You really know your wines."

"I'm no master sommelier. That's my cousin Andrea. But I fake it well." Her lips formed a mischievous grin. "Too bad you'll never know."

"Really? We'll have to see about that." When he laughed, warmth spread through Sierra, touching her soul. Oh, he was dangerous. Flirty yet serious. Attractive and debonair. James Bond mixed with the boy next door—a lethal combination. He winked and his devilish mouth twisted slyly. "And Sierra, just so you know, there's nothing to worry about. There's no way you'd ever have to fake it when you make it with me."

Chapter Nine

As Sierra's mouth closed over the rim of the wine glass containing the old vine Zinfandel, Jack worked to suppress a grin. With his comment on not having to fake it with him, he'd again rendered Sierra speechless. He had no regrets in raising any kind of reaction from her.

All hot and bothered himself—her lips should be outlawed—he wanted her as discombobulated as he was. Fair was only fair, right? His groin tightened for the millionth time since Saturday. A soft flush bloomed on her cheeks, creating a glow making her even more desirable than she'd been in high school. Then he'd thought her the cutest girl in school. Too bad his dumbass, myopic social set couldn't see anything beyond their own noses and tight inner circle. Too bad Jack hadn't realized said fact until too late—that he'd been the one hanging out in the wrong crowd.

With her wineglass safely planted back on the table, Sierra lifted her water bottle. Did she know the effect she had on him? She sipped deeply, as if the cold water could quench whatever was buzzing rocket fire between them. When she swallowed, the movement caused Jack to send half a bottle of water down his own throat, the icy liquid failing to quench the furnace firing inside him. He wanted her, that was clear. He could picture himself trailing kisses down her neck...

He set the wine bottle aside and retrieved the sandwiches. Eating was a good fail-safe, and if they were going to drink a glass of wine, they had to eat or this venue would be their last stop. He had so much more to show her and didn't want the day to end.

"Which sandwich do you want? This one is a turkey BLT with Havarti on a croissant. This one is a smoked pork with coleslaw and chipotle aioli on a Parmesan focaccia. If you don't like either of these, I'll have them bring out something else."

"They both sound delicious. I'll take the turkey. Unless you want it?"

"It's yours." He passed her the sandwich, then began removing containers of green grapes and carrot chips from the basket. "I chose easy finger foods to keep with the picnic theme. There are forks if you want them."

"Fingers work. Nice and simple." Sierra unwrapped her sandwich and placed it on the plate. She broke off a bunch of grapes and dumped out some carrots before passing him the containers.

He relaxed as the meal went on. He'd worried they might not make easy conversation, but like last night, before they'd gotten interrupted, they talked nonstop, starting with their favorite movies. Her cinema likes were varied and eclectic, and she revealed she'd seen most of the Oscar winners for best picture, including all the old classics. She refused to watch horror, and instead had a soft spot for romantic comedies. One of her all-time favorites was *You've Got Mail*.

"I didn't realize the premise was similar to *A Cinderella Story*, a movie my friends and I watched on repeat nonstop. Do you know the plot?"

He couldn't say that he had.

"Chad Michael Murray and Hillary Duff start conversations with each other online and they don't know each other's identity. She's not popular and he's the quarterback. In *You've Got Mail*, Meg Ryan's character hates Tom Hanks's. His Fox Books is putting her out of business but she's talking to him online and then he becomes her friend and, well, it gets complicated from there."

Jack sensed an underlying theme. He really had

been the asshole, hadn't he? "I'm not really a rom-com guy but I'm sure they fall in love and live happily ever after. That's the basic storyline, right?"

He'd caught the similarities to what had happened to them. Had added up all the clues she'd dropped, like watching *My Fair Lady* and then the teen version called *She's All That*. That had involved a bet regarding prom. Damn, he'd truly screwed up with Sierra. He hadn't been the hero she'd needed. He hadn't figured out the truth, unlike the guys in the movies who'd come to their senses. He'd been oblivious. Thinking she'd rejected him, he'd centered the blame on her. He'd thought she'd liked him until she'd rejected him, making him the fool.

"Chad Michael Murray is doing a lot of Hallmark Channel movies now. He's still got those good looks even though he's a decade older than me," Sierra said.

Jack blinked himself back into the conversation. "Then I'm glad he doesn't live in Beaumont so I don't have to be jealous. Although that sounds like the plot of a movie. Hollywood heartthrob sweeps away small-town girl."

"Yeah, trust me, that one's been done many times. My mom and I watch together. Sometimes Dad joins us."

Jack popped some grapes into his mouth. She was a badass fighter pilot with a secret soft side. He never would have pegged her for a romantic, yet he heard the hint of wistfulness, proving how much of a dunce he was. He didn't deserve a second chance, but now that he knew the truth about what happened, he wanted one. Heck, he'd wanted one even before knowing. She'd already gotten under his skin in more ways than one.

Too bad their first conversations in high school hadn't been anonymous. Maybe then she would have known the real him, and not the guy who existed on a popularity plane the selected, lucky few inhabited. He wanted to talk to her about high school. While he got the gist that there had been a bet, he wanted the whole story about what Paula and Randy had done. He wanted to make things right. He had to make amends. He wanted to kiss Sierra like they'd done once, see if the magic returned.

If time machines were real, he'd set the dial so he could return to high school and do everything over. However, since no one had yet discovered how to turn back time, Jack reminded himself to be patient. More than once, he'd been accused of being a human bulldozer. Some restraint wouldn't hurt when it came to wooing Sierra James. She was no pushover, nor did he want her to be. He had to convince her he was an upright guy, especially as he was trying to buy her family's winery and she was questioning him about the trees he'd removed.

"My company tries to be as environmentally friendly as possible. That's one thing I'm proud of, our record on land stewardship," he defended. "Even if we did take down some trees to create the view, we worked with a specialist to ensure that any old-growth timber went to the mill and that any brush was turned into mulch. Most of the trees here were elms, and many had that Dutch elm disease, so it made sense to take them down. If you look around, you'll see native plants. We don't import things that require constant watering. We want to do our part for the planet as well. We recycle everything, like that plastic in your hand, and I'm looking into washing our wine bottles."

"Good to know. Beaumont matters to me. So much has changed since I left. Now that I'm back, I want some things to be the same."

"I can understand that." He did. That was the tricky part about being a developer, trying to maintain the balance of the cherished old and the innovative and profitable new, all while being a good steward of the earth.

Sierra capped her empty water bottle. She gazed over the peaceful river valley before her brown-eyed gaze sought his. "This has been a nice lunch. Thank you for inviting me. I'm enjoying this."

Her compliment squeezed something inside his chest, creating a delightful pressure. He'd hardly slept, worrying about his plans, but in the end, he hadn't made any changes, including opting for a picnic instead of pizza. He capped his bottle. "I'm glad. I want you to enjoy today. Thanks for agreeing to go on this adventure and allowing me to show you my vision. It's fun seeing things through your eyes. I'm a firm believer in being out of the office as much as possible as I figure things out. Your presence helps. And you're good company. I'm glad we reconnected." Did he sound nervous? He swore he'd been babbling.

"Me too. But that doesn't mean I approve all your changes. I'm hoping you don't spoil the region's charm."

"I won't," he declared, even more determined not to after today. "I want to put Beaumont on the map and make wine country a year-round destination far beyond St. Louisans wanting to get lit for the afternoon. I'm not one of those developers who wants to come in and clear cut and bulldoze everything."

"Perhaps not, but how do private jets and eighteen holes designed by a golf legend fit into a quiet, lazy weekend afternoon? We're simple people. Beaumont is quaint and steady. You're high-end. This isn't Aspen or Lake Tahoe. A dinner yacht cruising the Missouri? What's that about?"

Even arguing with her felt oddly familiar. They'd debated so many things in high school and she'd challenged him in ways no one else had since, especially when she held her ground. "Have you been to either? Or on a cruise?"

"That's beside the point. Just because all your

fancy changes will create tons of profit doesn't make every single idea of yours right for the region."

She was passionate, he gave her that. "We aren't here to destroy but enhance. Visitors bring money. Why shouldn't Beaumont be the recipient of tourist dollars? Historic buildings require maintenance, as do cobblestones, asphalt and city parks. Why shouldn't those be funded using tourist dollars rather than increasing taxes on locals when the coffers are thin? My company plans to provide different levels of experiences. We aren't using tax-increment financing, and there will also be an immediate increase in revenue from sales taxes. We'll also be a big employer, and we pay well. I'm a firm believer in a living wage."

Finished with his spiel, he figured he must have proved his point when she didn't return fire. He was not a bad guy and wanted her to believe that.

She handed him her empty plate and glass, which he stored in the basket. "Fair enough. What's next on our agenda?"

He took her hand in his and helped her to her feet. Warmth fused their fingers, and they stood face-to-face, their mouths in a gap easily surmountable should either of them lean forward. Her lower lip dropped slightly. Her tongue darted out and swiped before disappearing. Her searching gaze held his. A gentle breeze blew, lightly teasing strands of rich brown hair that framed her face. Overhead a hawk yipped a distinctive cry, and fallen leaves rustled as an unseen small woodland creature moved through the undergrowth. Jack desired a kiss. At this moment, he wanted her lips under his more than anything else, including her winery. Instead Jack let Sierra's hand go and stepped back. Mixing business with pleasure was a line he didn't cross. But how he'd wanted to explore and taste her sweetness! Doing the right thing and following his personal code sometimes sucked. Today was one of those times.

He wrapped his fingers around the basket handles and forced a friendly yet mysterious smile. "Come on. I promised I'd show you the entire operation. Let's move on to what's next."

Chapter Ten

As she and Jack walked to the Mercedes to leave Primrose Hill, Sierra tried to control her trembling. Before Jack had broken their connection, she'd been holding his hand. It was obvious from the way his eyes had darkened and the poised tension in his jaw that he'd wanted to lean forward and kiss her. And, God forbid, had he inched toward her, she would have kissed him back.

What the hell was she thinking, wanting Jerk Clayton's lips on hers? But for an instant, until they'd each regained their senses, she'd craved the feel of his mouth. She'd longed to taste his kiss, to sample the reality that had tormented her since that one time in the library. He'd occupied each and every one of her teenage dreams. The adult version walking next to her was twice as deadly. Triple as seductive. Four times the fun. What had been a childhood crush was turning into unstoppable adult desire.

Wine. Drinking old vine Lodi Zinfandel had to have caused this temporary insanity. Even though she'd imbibed in one glass in the entire hour and a half they'd picnicked on Primrose Hill, and that had been at the start of lunch, she decided it had to be the effects of wine muddling her brain. The wine had softened her defenses, like all good red vintages tended to do. Alcohol was a depressant after all, with tons of addiction centers warning of its ability to impair judgment and lessen inhibitions.

She'd been addicted to Jack Clayton since elementary school. Her feelings had bordered on that fine line between love and hate for years. Hadn't she decided in kindergarten, in that game where all the girls decided who they'd marry, that she would marry Jack? Who cared that he was a second-grader? Or that he'd pulled on her hair? Or that boys had cooties? Not her. He'd been it, and until the bet, she'd always seen him through rose-colored glasses.

Thank God, unlike some of the popular girls who'd declared their intentions as if staking out a claim, Sierra had never told a soul, minus writing his name in her diary. The journal lay locked safely away inside a memory trunk in the basement of her parents' house. Buried at the bottom, the missive remained securely stowed under tons of other school-age memorabilia. She'd thought that she'd been a pathetic fool, crushing on such a jerk. Now uncertainty gathered. She wavered. The man aged like fine wine, damn him.

She happened to like fine wine, and Jack was proving to be a rare vintage.

He slid behind the wheel and reached into the center console. As he had at Elephant Rocks, he blew into a small device, noted the reading and dropped it back. "Good to go," he told her.

She gazed out the passenger window, lest he see her tumult. It was hard to hate a man who used a Breathalyzer to ensure he didn't drive impaired. High school was also long ago—this grudge she held seemed childish. Admittedly, she never made good choices with men. Best she remember Jack wanted to buy her dad's vineyard. Once he achieved his goals, he'd install managers in place and hightail it back to Portland. She was a temporary distraction. Maybe nostalgia was like an itch needing to be scratched.

The rest of the afternoon, the convertible wove through tree-lined highways as Jack took her to his other vineyards. They didn't do any tasting at those venues, but at each place he outlined his vision and took her on a tour. They even drove to the county park, to the concrete ramp where boaters launched into the Missouri River. Pink plastic streamers tied onto wooden stakes marked where his company would build the pier. The upcoming improvements also included an actual marina where boaters could purchase fuel, which would be a welcome addition to the region.

"We don't envision berthing large houseboats like those on the Mississippi as we want to keep this area simpler and more natural," Jack said. "We'll start with the yacht specially designed for sightseeing and dinner cruises and see how things go, but I doubt much else will change. Adding more than one yacht would destroy the charm. Ready?"

They turned from the water view, pausing as a diesel dually crew cab pickup backed down the boat ramp. Out in the river, a speckled red-and-black bass boat edged toward shore.

"Do you fish?" Jack asked.

"No. My brothers lived at our pond because Dad kept it stocked, but it wasn't my thing. I wasn't really into doing any deep-sea fishing either. Although eating fresh fish that's been tossed on the grill is badass delicious."

"You probably ate plenty of fresh seafood in Florida. Not as widespread here."

"I'll get used to being landlocked again." She used this as the opportunity to segue into his future plans and move the conversation away from her. They'd talked about tons of things today, making easy and fun conversation. She needed to re-mind her heart he was leaving. "Where are you headed next?"

"On to the next project, wherever that may be."

Did she hear a lack of enthusiasm? Didn't mat-ter. They had no future, and she should not even be thinking about that. "Speaking of projects, did you read Paula's email?" Sierra had skimmed it earlier after her breakfast with Emily.

"It sounds like a worthy endeavor," Jack hedged, an unspoken *but* in his voice.

"And?" she prompted. "You can tell me. Paula and I aren't friends."

"I'd rather write another check," Jack admitted with a sheepish smile. "It's how we normally spon-sor things. Throw money at them."

"That's how you do a lot of things." Sierra warmed to something Emily had mentioned during breakfast that morning, a way to get a little payback without being vicious. "It'll be good PR for you to put in some actual face time at the event. Let people see you as something more than a stuffy suit with deep pockets. Get your hands dirty in a good way."

They'd reached the convertible. "My hands aren't dirty in a bad way," Jack defended, holding them out for inspection. The car stood between them like a shield. "I don't make deals with unethical peo-ple. I know you're angry I want your winery, but

I wouldn't be underhanded in how I go about acquiring it."

She'd clearly pushed one of his buttons. "I meant you should do something aside from push paper or type on a keyboard."

"Ah, got it." Relief relaxed his features, making him even sexier in the afternoon light. If only he wasn't a nemesis, she'd throw caution to the wind and tell him to drive to the nearest hotel. No, she wouldn't do that actually, but she'd thought about it for a moment.

He gave her a sheepish smile. "Sorry. I get accused of a lot of bad things, but being underhanded and dirty is not one of them."

Sierra pressed on. "Getting involved will allow people to see you as a part of the community, not simply as an interloper buying land. Seriously, how hard would it be to staff the ring toss tent? Be approachable. You're a bazillionaire from the West Coast. People have the right to be suspicious of your intentions."

"Like you are."

She acknowledged that with a tilt of her head. "You are trying to buy my family's businesses. And I haven't seen you in a decade. Given what had happened in high school, I'm trying to reconcile the adult you with the one I knew."

He considered her, his fathomless gaze unreadable. Then his face morphed into determination. "That's fair. Fine. I'll do it."

"Great!" She couldn't wait to tell Emily.

"We'll do it together."

"No. Wait." This was not what she intended. He reached into his pocket and withdrew his phone. Tapped in his code instead of holding the device to his face to unlock it. He sent a quick email. "Done. I accepted on our behalf."

Panic bubbled. Spending even more time with him wasn't the plan. Had Emily planted the idea that Sierra encourage Jack to do the festival because Emily had known Jack wouldn't do it without Sierra? Surely her friend was not that devious or matchmaking, especially given the history. No, she and Sierra had totally misjudged Jack. "I'm not the one needing to be visible in the community. I'm not buying the place. You are. You need to be the one to do it."

Standing by the driver's door, he stared at her across the car. "You can help me navigate the political waters."

She slid onto the passenger seat. "I was gone, remember? I don't know the town politics. If I had, I wouldn't have made such a mess freshman year. You're better off going alone."

Jack shook his head. "I have no desire to do this without you. You said you are trying to reconcile the new me versus the old me. Working together will provide time for me to show you I'm not the same person. That I'm sorry for whatever happened. I liked you, Sierra. I really did. I never lied about that."

He'd liked her. Her heart leaped at the words. The driver's door closed with a strong click, but he made no move to put on his seat belt. Instead he faced her. "Paula and Randy have always been cocky, egotistical assholes, especially Randy. They believe they are big fish in a small town, always have and still do. I didn't realize their hypocrisy and shallowness, or how their social circle infected me into believing all that shit they spewed, until I was the new, random kid in a sea of faces in a far larger high school."

He'd stunned her. "Wow. Don't hold back."

His forehead creased as his mouth turned serious. "I never do. Not anymore. Will you finally tell me what happened? While I said this day was for business, it's four o'clock. Quitting time. Tell me what happened. I deserve to know. Please."

Sierra spread her fingers over her jeans. Until she wiggled out of it, they were about to be working together on the Halloween festival. She should clear the air, even if things would get awkward after. "You asked me to homecoming."

"Yeah, and you turned me down." He shifted impatiently, as if the plush leather underneath him was no longer comfortable. "That's old history. I took a lot of crap over the fact I asked a freshman and she said no."

"Because Randy had to refund all the money." The words rushed out—the fact there had been a bet still smarted. Teenagers could be mean, but until then she hadn't experienced the depths they'd go. She'd certainly never expected them to be heartless and vile. The revelation had been eye-opening, and she'd kept to herself for the remaining three years.

Jack scowled. "I'm starting to see the full picture. But clear it up for me."

"I liked you too. That kiss? Magical." She shifted. "When you first asked me, I wondered what you were thinking, asking a freshman. Despite the kiss, you were popular. Believing I was unworthy meant you had to have a deeper motive. Then Emily heard about the bet."

"I still don't quite understand. Who made a bet?"

"A group of your friends made a wager as to how long it would take for you get into my pants and take my virginity after the dance."

Jack whistled low. "That's cold. I'm so sorry."

"Emily heard you were in on it. I was rightfully devastated and turned you down. Thankfully I'd learned the truth long before I made a fool of myself by going with you and becoming another one of your conquests."

Jack's fingers dug into the leather-wrapped gear selector. He tensed his fingers before letting go. "I had no idea. I wasn't in on it. I wanted to take you to homecoming."

"Why? Why me when you could have had any girl? Pretty much had a few by that point, if the gossip about you and Lillian Passat was true." The whole school had talked about their adventures. Lillian had worn the attention like a badge of honor.

"Kissing you rocked my world. Maybe by then I wanted something real."

"Yeah, and pigs fly. You were leaving. Moving. How real was a dance going to be?"

Jack shrugged, as if trying to relieve tight shoulders. "No idea. It was something I wanted to do. I wanted to be with you."

She couldn't believe what he was telling her. "We hardly spoke if it wasn't for your math homework. You were my brother's friend, not mine."

"Maybe I wanted to be? Maybe I'm shy?"

She scoffed. "Please? You? You were Mr. Gregarious."

His scowl deepened. "Yes, dammit, I am shy where you're concerned. I've always been on shaky ground around you. You're smarter than me. Brighter. More determined. You didn't give a shit about me or my money or my social status. You never gave me the time of day unless it was to lord over me about why I couldn't get a problem correct. Call it an exercise in futility. You were a sunbeam that I wanted to hang around, and you wouldn't give me the time of day. Then when you reached high school, it was like *pow*. You were all I could see. And then we shared that kiss and it was game over."

"I can't quite believe that. You powed a lot of girls, Jack. You were always dating someone."

"You were two years younger. We weren't in the right place or even the same school for more than a year. Maybe I was waiting for you to grow up."

"That's an adult answer. You wouldn't know that as a junior in high school."

"Why not?" he challenged.

"Because teenagers are hormonal crazies. They have a crush on one person one day and then they've moved on to someone else the next. Or teenagers think they're in love and their date will be their soul mate for eternity, not realizing they've seen so little of the world that they don't even know who they are as a person, much less know what they truly want. Teenagers live in the moment."

"Well, maybe that day I felt I wanted to kiss you. And I'm glad we did. Maybe things would have been different had I been more aware of what my so-called friends said. But I liked you. I'll say it again. That was real."

She blinked. She'd been tutoring him in math, sitting at the local library in a back corner. She'd turned her head, and his lips had been right there— so close his soft exhale warmed her cheek. He'd been watching her face, not the math problem she'd been solving on scratch paper. They'd been inches apart, and time seemed to have frozen. She'd stared at his lips, much like she was doing now, noting the little ridges, the dip and the subtle hint of bottom teeth. Then Jack leaned to kiss her, and his lips on hers had been nothing like her first kiss with Bobby Reed after a night of roller skating when she'd been in seventh grade.

Sierra had been the one to break off from Jack's kiss that day, but not before she'd flushed all over and experienced a wildfire traveling head to toe, which had been accompanied by a tingly pressure at the juncture of her thighs. Sort of like how her body anticipated him now, in this moment. He'd moved closer, over the convertible's center console. If she shifted, she could bring her mouth to his. He smelled divine, all woodsy and male. She'd always pushed the envelope. What would one sip hurt?

"Sierra." His lips formed her name, and then he crossed the remaining distance and captured her lips with his.

Holy hell. The words flitted in and out as Jack's kiss overpowered all sense of reason, as if he'd detonated a dozen fireworks. He did nothing by half measures, and Sierra lost herself in a symphony of color and awe.

He nipped, tugged and flicked out his tongue, running the tip over her lips. He cradled her head in his palm and better angled his mouth over hers.

Her lips parted, and he took his time exploring. The earlier tingles became a needy ache. Her breasts felt heavy, longing to press against his chest as his fingers massaged the back of her neck. She stroked his strong jawline, the day's stubble prickly delicious. Taking more control, she sucked his tongue, emboldened by his growling groan of pleasure. She darted around his mouth, memorizing the texture—positively divine.

A series of honks interrupted, accompanied by "Woo-hoo! Get a room!" raucous catcalls shouted from the guys in the pickup. They drove by, bass boat in tow.

Sierra leaned against the passenger seat, mortified. She was sitting in a top-down convertible making out. Had she and Jack not been interrupted, how difficult would it have been to have shimmied off her jeans, slide down his zipper and settle onto his lap?

The thought of doing so made her heart race and her body tremble.

To her left, Jack shifted, adjusting himself. Sierra stared straight ahead at the grove of trees lining the edge of the parking lot. This was the only boat ramp in the county; people drove for miles to use it. She hadn't recognized the truck's occupants, who appeared to be in their late forties, far younger than her parents and much older than she or Jack, making the probability low they'd recognized her or Jack. Last thing she needed was more town gossip.

"Sierra." Jack's voice was gentle. "Sierra, look at me."

She couldn't hide from him forever, especially when sitting in his car. She turned her head.

He gave her a wary yet tender smile. "Wow."

Had he said anything else she might have lost it. Instead his words brought forth a series of giggles as tension fled. "Yeah," she admitted as the totality of the moment hit her. "That was a great kiss. Got a bit carried away there."

"I'd say." Tender fingers smoothed her hair into place. "I have no regrets about what just happened."

What could she say? She'd always wanted to kiss him again, and it hadn't disappointed. Left her instead craving more. Kissing him was like popping a cork on a bottle of champagne. You drank one glass and wanted another. But too much bubbly was always bad, as it left those who indulged hungover the next morning.

A falcon flew overhead, cawing for its friends. Sierra tried to make light. "Good thing we didn't go further in high school. You would have been in my pants and Randy would have won."

Jack cradled her cheek. "Had I known, I would have beaten the crap out of him. Still might. He deserves it."

His anger calmed her. "He's not worth breaking your hand. None of them are."

Jack blinked. "You're not still a…"

"Oh hell no," Sierra retorted. "With a guy I dated in the Academy. He's on the admiral track. We both went our separate ways. He's on a carrier somewhere in the Middle East on his way to being captain."

"He sounds impressive."

Sierra shrugged. "He had goals and ambitions, as did I. That was probably the basis of our attraction. We were seniors, both too committed to our careers to see ourselves as anything long term. Besides, there are all these rules and regulations in the Academy. Do an internet search and you'll find articles about complaints on social media about how difficult it is to find love when you're training as much as we do."

"And neither of you were rule breakers."

"Not when it came to our naval careers. But with you? Sitting here breaks all my rules."

His thumb stroked her cheek. "Why?"

"Because I don't make out in cars in the middle of the parking lot of a boat ramp. And certainly not with you." Especially as he was the boy who'd broken her heart and could do it all over again if she wasn't careful.

"I'd like to be with you," Jack said. "I don't know what the future holds, but I definitely want to make love to you. And that breaks all my rules of mixing business and pleasure."

"Well, that was coming right out in the open."

His thumb created a sensitized swish against the corner of her lip. "We had a communication problem in high school, so I'm not going to speak in euphemisms now. I want you. I'd like to take you out. We'd be great in bed and I'd love to see you naked and spread out beneath me. Hopefully that's clear enough."

"Very." She contemplated his words and the thrill his desire created within her. He started the car and the engine roared to life.

"I'm going to drive you home before I kiss you again. As for another time, that's up to you. I've made it clear what I want."

"I don't see how even something casual could work," Sierra said. Wait, was she seriously considering it? "You're trying to buy my parents' vineyard, which they aren't going to sell, and I'm not going to let them anyway, so—"

"Our being together would be about hanging out and having a good time, not business," Jack interrupted. "You, Sierra, would be all pleasure."

If he kept up the seduction, she would need to release herself later from this sexual madness. He'd always driven her crazy, and today he'd handed her an offer of no-strings sex. She should be insulted, but instead she found herself intrigued. If the kiss today was an indicator, making love with Jack would be extraordinary. Mind blowing. Passionate. Focused on her career, she'd slept with only one man, so her experience was limited. Spending some nights with Jack, and learning how her body could respond, had both sexual and clinical appeal. After all, one should learn from a master.

"What are you thinking about?" he asked, as if trying to read her mind.

"I'm thinking I'm a modern woman so I'm weighing my options. When I decide I'll let you know."

He shot her a sideways glance, but he'd put on sunglasses against the late afternoon sun so she couldn't read his expression. Sierra resisted texting Emily. She wasn't going to believe this turn of events.

He turned into her driveway, slowing the car to a crawl over the gravel. He parked on the concrete pad. "I'm serious, Sierra. The decision is yours. We could be good together."

Before she could answer, her dad, upon hearing the car, came out of his garage, chamois in hand. "Hi, Dad."

"Nice Mercedes," her dad said instead.

"Thank you." Jack did the polite thing and got out of the car to shake her dad's hand. "I'm Jack."

"Good to meet you, Jack."

Was it? Sierra hoped her dad was having one of his better days.

"I didn't realize you'd be home already," Sierra said. Her mom usually picked her dad up from his adult day care before five. Sierra glanced at her watch. It was ten minutes until six. Where had the day gone?

"Hi, Sierra." Her mom appeared on the porch.

"Mom, this is Jack. Jack Clayton. From high school? I tutored him in math? And he's the one wanting to buy your winery? Bought all the others, remember?"

"Hello, Jack." Her mom's welcoming smile didn't falter, but Sierra recognized an underlying hint of curiosity in her pleasant tone.

"Nice to meet you, ma'am." Jack held out his hand politely as her mom joined them. Her mom wrapped his palm in both of her hands before adding a small shake.

"Call me Jayne. This is Marvin." As Jack's arm returned to his side, Sierra's mom turned to her husband. "Were you working on your cars? I wondered where you'd gone."

Her father was running his hand over the front of Jack's Mercedes. "How much horsepower is under this hood?"

"Enough to get the job done," Jack said.

Her father made a disappointed noise. "You should know if you're going to drive a beauty like this."

Jack used his phone to internet search. "Three hundred sixty-two. It's a turbocharged inline-six with EQ Boost."

Her dad wiped a spot with his cloth. "They can

do so much with a V6 these days that used to take a V8. Have you ever seen my cars?"

Uh-oh, Sierra knew where this led. "Dad…"

"I've heard about them," Jack said. "I'd love to see them."

"This way." Her dad pointed and Jack fell into step. Keeping a careful eye on the two men, Sierra and her mom followed at a distance. Inside his garage, her dad was in his element. His brain remained sharp and clear when talking about his cars. Jack, to his credit, did more than feign interest. He was an active participant, especially when it came to sitting in her dad's most precious mechanical baby, the Shelby Cobra. Jack ran his fingers over the steering wheel and smiled. "You ever want to sell this, you call me first."

"Ah, son, you don't have the money," her dad said affably, his pride evident.

Jack rose in Sierra's estimation when he didn't contradict her dad and tell him that yes, he did have the funds. Buying the car would be a mere drop from Jack's overflowing bucket. Jack reluctantly exited the car and gently closed the door. "These are great cars. I can see why you love them. They're beautiful. Well, I should probably get going."

"You're not staying for dinner?" Her mom turned to Sierra, as if her daughter had failed to be hospitable.

"I, uh, we've been together since eleven and I wasn't sure what Jack had planned. I…"

"I was explaining my vision for Beaumont today," Jack added helpfully. "We toured all the wineries my company purchased and stopped by the boat ramp."

Sierra caught the gleam in Jack's eye and heard the undertone when he referenced the boat ramp. Her dad, however, heard his second favorite word other than *cars* and lit up with interest. "Wine? Did you say you make wine? I own a winery."

"He owns Primrose Hill and Elephant Rock," Sierra told her dad. "Along with a few others."

"Huh. Didn't know that old Masters sold out. He always was a fool. What's your favorite vintage?" As they left the garage, her dad set the alarm. "I'm partial to the Norton myself."

"I've had your Norton, sir, and no one makes it the way you do."

Her dad grinned. "They certainly don't."

Jack and her dad began to talk wine during the walk to the house, and Sierra put her hand on her mom's arm so that she paused. "Are you sure this is wise? Having him in for dinner? He's trying to buy the winery. What if he figures out Dad's not all there?"

"Sierra." Her mom used the tone that said any argument was a wasted effort. "We will not hide your dad's condition. Jack can make as many offers as he wants. He has to do his job. We'll do ours and be hospitable."

"What if he convinces Dad to sell to him? What if Dad decides he likes him?"

Her mom showed no concern. "Then we'll cross that bridge when we come to it, as we have at every other juncture of our marriage. You don't need to worry about us."

Sierra did worry. She could see how much of a toll her dad's illness took. Her mom had lost weight and had tiredness ringing her eyes. But her mom's character remained firm.

"Jack, do you like meat loaf?" her mom asked. "Tonight is meat loaf, mashed potatoes with all the fixins and a blueberry cobbler for dessert."

Jack's eyes lit up. "Homemade cobbler?"

"Is there any other kind?"

Jack gave Sierra's mom the grin that had been charming women since the day he was born. "No, ma'am. Especially when I've heard you're the best cook in the county. I'd be honored to stay, if Sierra agrees."

He'd trapped her. No way would she play the bad guy tonight. Sierra spread her hands in a welcome gesture. "Please join us for dinner."

Jack's satisfaction threatened to suck her in and never let her go. "I'm delighted to accept."

Chapter Eleven

Jack had eaten at some of the finest establishments in the world. His work owning hotels, restaurants, wineries and so forth required it. For grins, he was halfway through visiting the top Michelin star restaurants in the United States. He'd seen food plated so beautifully and cooked so expertly his mouth watered before he'd even lifted a fork.

All those meals paled compared with the simple, flavorful, home-cooked meal Sierra's mom placed in front of him. On a dining room table set with mismatched colors of Fiesta dinner plates, he served himself multiple slices of succulent meat loaf, a heap of mashed potatoes that were so light and fluffy they melted in his mouth and a juicy cob of late summer corn. Mrs. James added hot brown gravy, fresh-baked bread with butter and homemade applesauce. By the end of the meal, he could do with unfastening the top button of his pants, he'd eaten so well. And how could he resist cobbler topped with homemade vanilla bean ice cream?

"Thank you again," he said, his empty plate a badge of honor. "This has been exceptional. You could expand your cookie business and open a restaurant, this meal was so good."

"I'd blush but I'm too old. But I'll take the flattery." Sierra's mom laughed and waved off Jack's offer to help clear the table of dishes. "I've got this." She gave Sierra a pointed look. "Sierra, you should show him the fairy garden."

Jack's brow wrinkled. "Fairy garden?"

Sierra stood, neither unhappy nor happy. She gestured. "This way."

Jack followed her from the table. Whatever this garden was, it would give him a chance to speak with her before he left. Sierra removed a sweater from a hook by the screen door before leading him outside. The night was cool and crisp. "Where we're going isn't really a fairy garden, but a part of the flower garden that gets illuminated. It's easier to see than explain. Not sure why she wants me to show you this, but I'm not answering to her if I don't."

She led him down a stone path and toward a thick line of arborvitae. They went through a small gap between two of the trees, and once through, entered a small clearing.

"This is my mom's folly." Sierra went to a metal pole about waist high. At the top was a standard outdoor electrical box. She opened the cover plate, pressed a button and immediately hundreds of tiny white Christmas-style lights lit the space.

The fairy lights revealed four curved concrete benches. They surrounded a ten-foot-diameter pond edged with natural stones. Orange koi fish swam in the darker water. Behind one of the benches, set off a way, was a wooden swing. "What a great space," Jack complimented.

"Thanks. Dad has his garage, the boys had the pond, and my mom claimed this. She comes out here to think and get away from everything, and I've started doing the same since I got back. It's peaceful."

"It's beautiful." Deep forest air filled his lungs as he broached the subject of her dad. "How long has your dad been like this?"

"Like what?" She pretended to be confused.

He gently called her out. "Sierra. We're trying to be honest in our communication, remember?"

"True." Resignation claimed her and her shoulders slumped. "And we don't hide it. It's early onset and it started a few years back. He's part of a clinical trial, and we're hopeful. But..."

He empathized. "My grandfather had Alzheimer's. It was hard to watch. I can't even imagine what you're going through with it being your dad. I was much more removed. My parents were the front line. I was off in college."

"You can understand why selling is not high on our priority list. We have other issues."

"Yes." He did, but that didn't make his desire for their land and vines abate. If nothing else, he saw their selling as a solution to many of their problems, especially the ones he knew would come when Marvin's health degraded further. Instead of seeing their outright rejection as a ploy for more money or a better offer, Jack surmised they hadn't even considered his offer because of a lack of time, and a need to keep everything stable for her father.

Of course they wouldn't want to sell. Change would be very hard for Mr. James—he knew that from his grandfather's experience. Jack would have to think of a new approach, one that helped everyone get something they wanted. That was how to succeed in business—figure out what people needed and could live with.

But after a fabulous meal and an even better day, talking business with Sierra seemed sacrilegious in this romantic space. Especially as he'd love to kiss her again.

She sat on the wooden swing and he joined her, resting his back against the slats. They rocked back and forth without speaking, listening to the night.

A barn owl hooted. Animals rustled leaves. The koi pond gurgled. Sierra shivered as if the sweater wasn't enough and he settled his arm comfortably on her shoulders. She fit easily to him, which he liked. Above their heads, a fast flicker of light indicated the International Space Station cruised by. "That was cool. Don't see that often," he said, the silence accentuating his nervousness. He had much he wanted to say. He wanted to kiss her more. "You can't see the stars where I live because of the bright lights of the city."

To his delighted surprise, she snuggled closer and put her hand onto his chest. "I love it here. I hated it and wanted to get away, but this is always home, you know?"

He didn't know. His family had houses and hotels, not homes. No place he traveled or stayed had ever screamed *family* the way the James homestead did. "My family's not like yours. Houses are places to stay for a while, or places to store stuff and hold parties."

Her soft gaze captured his. "That's sad. I never thought I'd pity you, but I think I do."

He'd told her something personal, something he'd never shared with anyone, and tried to undo the danger. "Great. Not what I wanted at all."

She put her hand on his thigh and he swore he could feel the heat of her palm through his pants.

"Don't worry. Your secret is safe. You can be real with me. It's a nice change."

"You never thought me real before?" That bothered him.

"It was high school. None of us know who we are at that age. But you were too worried about what others thought of you. I liked you, but I didn't like you at the same time."

He'd already decided he'd been sort of an ass. Not Randy level, but guilty all the same of bad behavior. "True. Yours was the opinion that really mattered, though."

She blinked. "I never gave you my opinion."

"No, but I watched how you acted. You always marched to the beat of your own drum. You had such confidence, even back then. It was refreshing."

She sighed. "The truth is I faked it well. People consider coloring outside the lines bad. Eccentric. I wanted to be a sailor, God forbid. I was an oddball. So I leaned in."

He shifted his arm to draw her tighter. "Most people are pretty stupid, especially when they're in high school. I wish I'd been wiser. More of the guy you needed."

Something rustled in the trees. "No worries, I doubt it's a black bear," Sierra said. "Even though the population is really growing, especially farther south. If it is, I'm trained military. I'll protect you."

The creature was probably a deer, and Jack was

grateful its appearance lightened the moment. He caught Sierra's teasing tone. "You will, huh? You'll wrestle it with your bare hands. Ooh look, I made a pun."

"Aren't you clever?" She jabbed him in the ribs.

"Oof. Of course I am. I'm here with you, aren't I?" His fingers in perfect position, he began to tickle her. To his delight, she shrieked and tried to tickle him back. The result was they both landed in a thump on the soft, dewy grass, with Sierra on her back and Jack poised above her. "I'm going to kiss you now," he told her, bringing his lips closer to hers.

She met him halfway.

He explored her mouth, tasting cobbler and cream and a flavor uniquely hers that was sweeter than any nectar. Safely hidden from the house by the thick evergreens, he trailed kisses down her neck and into the hollow at the base of her throat. She stroked his back, and he ignored how part of him strained against his zipper. Balancing on one arm, he moved aside the sweater and unbuttoned her shirt. He pushed the cotton cloth aside to find a devastatingly sexy black bra. He moved the cup down and replaced it with his hand. The movement sent a jolt through him.

She arched her back, and he kneaded gently before lowering his mouth to the straining nub he'd craved forever. At last his lips surrounded her nipple. Pleasure shot straight to his groin as his brain registered one thing: Sierra was like tasting heaven. He flicked his tongue before gently blowing and tugging. When he repeated the process on her other breast, she gave a small kittenish cry.

He shifted to his opposite arm and moved his free hand to the juncture of her thighs and she bucked. He resisted the urge to tug down her zipper and slide a finger inside her heat. He first wanted to savor and enjoy this moment, not race to the finish line. He loved on her breasts and rubbed through her jeans until her legs shook and she gave a slight cry. He smiled to himself, pleased. One.

Many more orgasms to come if he got his way. But not necessarily tonight.

He returned his lips to hers and kissed her even more deeply before he drew back. "I should go."

"Go?" She stared at him with dilated eyes of hazy afterglow.

"Yeah. Go." He smiled softly. She was so beautiful. "It's late and I don't want our first time making love to be on a forest floor. Even if it's got the most romantic lighting ever and I want nothing more than to slide down your jeans and taste you."

He kissed her nose. "But let's not make your parents wonder if we're out here having sex like high schoolers who can't find a bed." He shook slightly as desire overwhelmed. "Damn, I want nothing more than to be inside you." He ached for her, as the bulge pressing against his denim showed.

"You didn't... Oh. I feel bad."

"It's not about me getting anything," Jack reassured. "I'll be fine. It's about our first time not feeling like a roll in the hay, or in this case, the wet grass."

He helped her to a sitting position, and she repositioned her bra and rebuttoned her shirt. He brushed a few pieces of broken leaves and blades of grass from her hair. "You are beautiful, you know."

"I don't know. But thanks. I'll walk you to your car." Sierra turned the lights off, plunging the small glade into darkness. His eyes adjusted and Jack took her hand in his as they headed back.

"Is this where we do the awkward 'I'll text you' thing?" Sierra asked when they reached his car.

"No, it won't be awkward because we *will* text. We're working on the Halloween festival together and I plan on seeing much more of you."

"You don't have to do the festival. Really, sending a check's enough. We can skip it."

He tipped her chin and gave her one last quick kiss before he slid behind the wheel. "But I want to because I'm doing it with you. Good night, Sierra. Sweet dreams."

Chapter Twelve

As Jack drove away, Sierra remained rooted until the red taillights faded in the distance like a spent firefly. Her parents sat in the front room watching TV, meaning Sierra slipped upstairs without disturbing them or subjecting herself to any questions. The mirror in the bathroom revealed she was a wreck. She plucked a spear of grass from her disheveled hair. Her lips appeared swollen from Jack's kisses. She'd fastened the buttons wrong and one shirttail hung lower than the other. She'd orgasmed from his mouth on her breasts and his hands on the outside of her jeans. He'd manipulated her body as if it were putty, turning her into a limp noodle. If this was a prelude to the full show… Sierra's anticipatory shiver ran from head to toe.

She tossed her phone on her bed. She'd had it on silent, and she swiped and read a text from Emily: How did today go? Did you survive?

The answer was she'd thrived. Come alive. Shattered, actually.

She'd kissed Jack. He'd had his mouth on her breasts. His touch had been everything she'd dreamed. And he said he wanted more.

Therein lay the problem. Sierra's head was already a hot mess. Jack hadn't known about the bet. He'd threatened to beat up Randy like some knight in shining armor. He'd always liked her. He wanted to make love to her. He'd offered a casual affair. But could she trust him? Jack had a prefixed agenda, which was to buy her parents' winery, build a regional wine destination and then leave. He might not be guilty of the high school incident, but he wasn't innocent of motive today either. She refused to be part of some master plan. No matter how many orgasms she might have.

Unsettled by the evening's activities and starting to doubt the blissful afterglow, she ignored Emily's text. She didn't want to admit to her best friend what she'd done with Jack. Maybe tomorrow she'd spill the beans. Sierra opened up her laptop. Her fingers trembled, but being with Jack had proved one thing. It was time to move forward. She answered the email from Boeing and accepted their job offer.

There. She'd done it. She had until January 3 to

get her shit together and manage her PTSD. She didn't expect to be 100 percent cured in two months. But she did believe she could learn to manage her symptoms as many others had. While the wreck and its aftermath would always be part of her past, the incident didn't have to define her future. She could move forward. However, saying those words and acting on them was easier said than done. Hence, intensive therapy.

Her phone rang, and Sierra sighed and swiped.

"You really should turn off the read receipts if you don't want me to think you're ignoring me," Emily said when Sierra answered. "When you ignore me that normally means stuff happened."

"I'm trying to gather the guts to tell you exactly what happened," Sierra admitted.

"Oh God. What did you do? Tell me you did not have sex with the man."

"No!" Sierra denied as heat spread through her. "Well, not all the way. But he knows me far more intimately than before."

"Sierra." Emily's warning was clear.

"I know. I know. But I couldn't help myself. Well, I could but—" The words rushed out. "We kissed down by the boat ramp. That's it."

"I sense there's a *but*." Emily's tone bordered on indignation mixed with curiosity. "You forget I know you well enough to know when you're either lying or hiding something. Spill the rest."

"He ate dinner with my family. Then before he left, we were out in the fairy garden talking—"

"Why were you in the fairy garden?" Emily demanded.

"My mom told me to show it to him."

"Uh-huh. Your mom left you alone with Jerk Clayton."

"It surprised me too." Sierra still didn't understand her mother's matchmaking ways, but she'd be mortified to ask her reasons. "Then he kissed me and—"

"He kissed you." Emily shrieked the words. "And you let him? Again?"

The words burst forth in a fast rush like water overrunning a dam. "Yes. He kissed me all over. Well, almost. And I loved it."

"Oh, girl, you're in deep trouble."

"I know. He's always been my kryptonite. Is it wrong that I wanted to know how he would make me feel? I'm a grown woman. I can have a sex life if I want one. And he's hunky. Even though my jeans stayed on, it was so good." In fact, her breasts remained sensitized.

"Did what happened mean to him what it meant to you?" Leave it to Emily to get to the heart of the matter. Sierra refused to tell her about Jack's offer for casual sex.

"It didn't mean anything to me," Sierra insisted a bit too vehemently.

"Liar. You'll fall for him all over and he'll break your heart. That's the last thing you need right now."

As she had for years, Emily called things the way she saw them. "This is why I didn't text you back," Sierra protested.

"Because I'm the voice of reason?"

"Exactly. I wanted to bask in the glow longer. It felt good. Like for once, I had everything."

"That man is like your mom's chocolate cake. Every bite is delicious but no way is all that sugar good for your health. Moderation matters."

"I know," Sierra admitted. "But why can't I indulge? At least once? He'll be leaving at some point so what would it matter in the long run?"

"If you think you can handle a no-holds, no-strings fling with Jerk Clayton, I'm not going to stop you. You deserve to have some wild, wicked sex. Take him for a roll. But don't you dare let him hurt you. Don't you dare fall for him."

"My eyes are wide open." Sierra made the promise with her fingers crossed. "I'm not letting him hurt me again. But I should tell you something."

Sierra filled Emily in on what she'd learned about Jack and the bet. "Maybe he did like you," Emily conceded. "But that doesn't forgive what happened."

"I was the nerdy girl with braces and no fashion sense," Sierra said. "I didn't fit in. But he saw through that."

"Sweetie, don't make me drive over there and

smack you out of this dream world. Jack might not have been part of it, but that doesn't make him Mr. Right. He isn't staying in Beaumont. You are."

"Sort of. I accepted the Boeing job. I'll eventually have to move to St. Louis County unless I want to keep the long commute."

Emily squealed. "That's great. About darn time."

"I agree. I've got to get myself together, and knowing I have a deadline will help. It's a great opportunity and I'm excited to be doing something that will hopefully make things better and safer for all the military pilots whenever they're in the air."

"You're going to do great. When do you see him again?"

"I don't know." Sierra picked at some lint on the bedspread. "He didn't say. Do I text him first? He said we'd text, but—"

"No." Emily's emphatic response came through loud and clear. "Absolutely not. Do not appear smitten or desperate. Be a challenge."

"I don't like playing games." She and Jack had also said they'd be honest with each other. Sierra flicked the lint onto the floor. She'd sweep later. "Why are things so complicated?"

"Because you're too much in your head. Today he threw you for a loop. You learned he was serious about you. But that was years ago. It's been over a decade. People change."

"I've told myself all this."

"I'm telling you, too, because that's what friends do. I only want you to be happy."

"I know," Sierra said. "I want to be happy too. I deserve it."

"Yes, you do," Emily reassured her before they said their goodbyes. Sierra ended the call. She'd always been the girl to try something once, as long as it wasn't illegal or too farfetched. Life was about adventure, which was one reason she'd loved flying. The next time she saw Jack might be as awkward as all get-out. But one thing remained crystal clear. She wanted more. She wanted the entire fantasy.

If only for one night.

Chapter Thirteen

Sierra didn't see or hear from Jack until Thursday. For a guy trying to get into her pants, he was doing a lousy job. She was burning up.

Not with passion and pleasure, however, but with anger and rage. Three full days. She hadn't heard from him in three days. And the more time stretched, the more she'd refused to be the one to break down and text him. A woman had her pride.

"I'm seriously annoyed to no end," Sierra told Emily as they walked into Jamestown for the monthly wine dinner. "Next time I tell you I kissed him, smack me silly. He wants me? Yeah, right."

"Hopefully he had something come up. I'd hate to have to hurt him. I'm sure, though, he has a good reason for not being in contact." Emily was always the optimist and the enforcer.

Sierra was the impatient one, especially when she'd been itching to get into the air and fly. But any great pilot always did due diligence, no matter how long those preflight checks took. "You won't have to hurt him because I'll beat you to it. Maybe he broke all his fingers and couldn't type. Then neither of us have to hurt him."

Although, Jack's fingers being broken would be a shame, especially since they could work magic. She'd lived on the residual high until midmorning Wednesday, when it was obvious he wasn't texting.

Sierra tried to hold back her anger but couldn't help releasing sarcasm. "But these days you can dictate and Siri will transcribe it into a text message. I'm not buying any excuses. He's as untrustworthy now as he was then."

"I told you not to get in over your head," Emily said as she and Sierra followed the hostess to a two-top table close to the windows. "Oh look, there's your cousin Andrea with Caleb. When did she get back in town? We should go over and say hi. I've followed her on Instagram ever since last June."

"She came to dinner with us last night," Sierra said before she nudged Emily. Anger laced her tone. "Maybe we should say hi to Jack first. See, he's right over there."

Emily's gaze followed the direction of Sierra's elbow. Emily made a slight noise. "Ooh, not cool. What a jerk."

"Which is what I'm going to tell him."

Jack sat at an intimate table closer to the fireplace, Taylor across from him.

Sierra paused as Emily placed her hand on Sierra's forearm. "Not now. Not here."

Recognizing it was not the time or place to confront him, Sierra plopped down into her chair. The fire blazed both in the hearth and in her veins as anger boiled. "You're right. I will not make a scene at my family winery. But, I am not going to be a sidepiece."

"No. Wait until you're alone and then give him hell. I'll even help you germinate a plan."

"Your last plan has me having to prep for the Halloween festival this weekend." Sierra reached for the filled and waiting water glass. She took a long sip, steadying her racing adrenaline. Storming over there would show Jack he'd gotten under her skin, that she cared about what they'd done together. Best to play tonight like she hadn't thought about his mouth fusing to hers. She'd pretend her orgasm hadn't meant anything because it clearly hadn't to him.

"Thanks for being such a good friend," she told Emily. "Confronting him like some hellfire would not be productive. But I don't like being used."

"No, and you shouldn't let him get away with it. But before you get all steamed, let's look at this logically. You've actually got him where you want him."

Sierra straightened and fingered the empty wine-glass. "How? Do tell because I certainly can't see it, not when I want him six feet under."

"That's because you're angry. Which is good. You're again seeing who he is without blinders, same as you did in high school."

"I don't see how this is helpful," Sierra said. She craned her neck and looked for their server. She could use that first wine pour.

"It's simple. You hold all the cards. He's got to work with you for the Halloween festival. He wants the winery. He wants you. Your choice what to give him. My opinion, don't give him squat. Make him realize what he's lost, again. Be the one woman he can't have."

"He's had me."

Emily used the expression that could freeze her twins midstride. "Not all of you. And he can't have your heart."

"Or the rest of my body. I've been letting my body get its way and not thinking straight. I'm thinking like a starry-eyed simpleton." Which was the exact opposite of how the military had trained her. Like chess, she had to outmaneuver until her combatant had no moves left. She would not let Jack checkmate her king. She had to be strategic. Calm. Controlled. He might be clever, but she was smarter, more determined, and she had more at stake.

Emily set down the placard outlining the night's

food courses. "You're scowling. Fix your face before he sees it."

Caught studying Jack and Taylor, Sierra smoothed her features. "How many units do you think she uses to get that brow lift?"

Emily gave a quick glance. "She's definitely enhanced her face with a few units and she uses some sort of filler in her lips. At least ten units for what she's had done. It's all the rage, even with women who are in their twenties. There's nothing wrong with a woman wanting to be beautiful. But can we not talk shop tonight?"

"I'm sorry. I'm annoyed so I'm being catty. I know better. But still, how would I compete with that, if I wanted to? I can't. No amount of fillers can turn me into a ten and a half like her." Sierra sighed and plucked at the linen tablecloth. "I'm not so much jealous as I am pissed off. I'm not sure what I want where he's concerned, and because of that, I'm ruining dinner, and they haven't even brought our first wine."

"Don't downplay your qualities. You are a beautiful and amazing Naval Academy graduate with a successful career."

"I appreciate that, but this is starting to feel like high school two-point-one. I'm the ugly duckling who will never become a swan. She'll be the one married to the dream man with perfect kids jetting off to Bali, while I'm a washed-up pilot who can't get her shit together to fly."

"Far from it. You need some time to recover, that's all. But Jerk Clayton—" Emily used the fitting nickname they'd given him "—is doing a number on your head. That needs to stop."

"Are you sure I can't go over and confront him? Perhaps dump a glass of water on him like in the movies?" Even as she spoke, Sierra knew what she proposed was a stupid idea, but voicing her anger at least got the emotion out into the open where she could control it. "Thanks for listening. I don't know what I'd do without you. You're a great friend and I don't deserve you."

"I know. But I love you anyway." Emily spoke with the confidence of one who'd been by Sierra's side through teenage zits and first crushes. They'd been there for each other always, good times and bad. Sierra had stood next to Emily when she'd married Jeff, and she served as a godmother to their twins.

Sierra's mood lightened. "He's not worth it," she declared.

"No," Emily agreed as their waiter arrived with their first wine pour. "No, he is not."

Chapter Fourteen

Jack shouldn't have agreed to attend the Jamestown wine dinner tonight. Not after what had happened between him and Sierra Monday evening. Seeing her tonight across the way, Jack knew he'd made a big mistake in not canceling. He'd recognized that indisputable fact when he'd watched Sierra enter the winery, glance his direction and then, with her head held high, pretend she hadn't seen him. He hadn't missed the thunderclouds flare before she'd controlled her expressions and turned poker-faced.

He knew how bad his sitting with Taylor appeared. For a man all about optics, Jack had no one to blame but himself for this unfortunate turn of events.

"Jack?" Across the table, Taylor bestowed an engaging smile. He hadn't seen much of Taylor this week, especially since he'd left for Portland Tuesday at 5:00 a.m. following the summons from his dad that had been waiting in Jack's inbox. He'd left Sierra's, caught a few hours of shut-eye and boarded the private plane. Today he'd retrieved his car from long-term parking about two hours ago, swung by the B&B serving as home base, retrieved Taylor and come straight here. He still wore the white button-down he'd had on during the board meeting, although he'd shucked the power tie and suit jacket and left them in the back seat. His suitcase remained in the trunk. His new phone—he'd dropped his and fried it—was in his pocket. He hadn't reached out to Sierra. He should have.

He focused on Taylor, not wanting to ruin her night—after all, she'd purchased the tickets when they'd been at the winery last Sunday. Jack had promptly forgotten about promising to attend. After the magical evening he'd spent in the fairy garden with Sierra, joining his PA for dinner had been the furthest thing from his mind and low on his list of priorities. Two days of meetings with his father and the board had been overwhelming and draining.

Add to that the fact that on Tuesday morning, when he'd left for Portland with the memory of Sierra on his lips, he'd received an email from his private investigator. Reading the dossier on the plane had made Jack feel dirty. Underhanded. Sleazy. All those things he railed against and prided himself

on not being. When he'd finished reading, he knew
things about Sierra's family even she didn't know.

Like how her father's treatment was bankrupt-
ing the family. Once the experimental drug trial her
dad had participated in had ended, her mother had
been buying the medication from abroad since the
drug wasn't approved in the United States. Three
months ago, they'd leveraged the winery for an influx of cash.

Jack wished her family had accepted his first
offer. If they had, he wouldn't have dug into the rest
of their lives. Doing due diligence was a common
business practice, Jack consoled himself, as if his
actions justified knowing private information about
the woman he'd brought to heaven in a fairy garden.
He hadn't planned on anything physical happening
between them, and he'd ordered the dossier long before he'd first kissed Sierra. But now, after he knew
about it, he'd been the one to make the choice to read
the file. He'd never felt shame before. He did now
and hadn't yet figured out what to do about solving
the vexing problem before him. He needed Sierra's
winery and he needed Sierra. He had to figure out
a way to have both.

People said all was fair in love and war, and business was both. But Jack prided himself on not being
cutthroat. He made fair, market-based offers. Eventually, those whose properties were in his sights
came around to the indisputable logic of selling.

The acquisition of Jamestown was different. Jack had eaten dinner with Sierra's parents. He'd compromised his impartiality. Let himself care. He liked Sierra and enjoyed being with her. He wanted her far more than the woman sitting across from him, whose hopeful expectations Jack knew he had to dash.

Worse, reading the report had given him Sierra's full backstory, something he wished she'd trusted him enough to share with him. Until he'd read the report, he hadn't realized she'd survived a plane crash, one caused by her student's error. She'd managed to save them both and she and her student had ejected from the fighter jet before it crashed. While no one on the ground was injured, both pilots had been. Sierra's student had become tangled in power lines; he'd touched live wires. He was lucky to be alive, and had been in critical care for months.

Sierra had also been in the hospital, but she'd fared better—as if having moderate injuries was the definition of *better*. With the exception of a broken leg, the investigator hadn't been able to access the full details or extent of her injuries. Jack allowed his gaze to wander over to where Sierra sat with Emily, who had always hated him. Emily's dislike made much more sense since Jack's discovery that she'd been the one to learn about the bet and warn Sierra.

Jack willed Sierra to glance his direction, but her head remained solidly in profile, as if she was deliberately ignoring his existence. This felt like high school all over again and he didn't like it one bit.

The waiter came by with a surprise, off-menu course, placing before Jack a tarte fine covered with tomatoes, goat cheese and romesco sauce. The presentation rivaled that of a high-end, Michelin star restaurant, which reinforced why Jack wanted to buy this winery. No one in the area did food like Jamestown.

"Jack," Taylor prodded. "Did you hear what I said? You seem a million miles away tonight."

"Sorry. Long day and flight back, you know." He attempted to concentrate on the story she was telling, something involving some mutual friends of theirs doing something somewhere, but as his mind drifted, all he could manage was the occasional "uh-huh" and "interesting" of conversational engagement.

Taylor deserved the truth, that what she wanted from him wasn't going to happen. He'd hired her because of his parents. His mom and dad couldn't have been more obvious that they'd love to see him date Taylor. She'd fit him and his lifestyle perfectly, they'd pressed, and she'd be the right type of society wife. He wasn't going to be in Beaumont forever, they'd reminded him, just long enough to get the project started. While they planned to spend time in Missouri post-retirement, Jack would run the Portland office. He was also needed to supervise their expansion into Washington State next summer.

Jack kept reminding himself all these things. Whatever he felt for Sierra, he had responsibilities that kept him from focusing on anything but work. But marrying a woman he didn't love wasn't a lifetime commitment he planned to make, even to please his beloved parents.

As beautiful as Taylor was, she didn't stir Jack's libido one iota. Plus, he was her boss.

Around Sierra he had to fight to keep his lower half in check. But what could he give her besides outstanding lovemaking? She had a job waiting for her. She belonged here.

Jack didn't. As recently as this morning's breakfast, Jack's dad had reinforced his eagerness for his eldest son to finish the purchases. Jack had been on the receiving end of a long lecture about how unhappy his dad was that Jack hadn't yet secured Jamestown. His father's "What are you waiting for, paint to dry?" had been warning enough.

Jack might get away with upsetting his father by refusing to marry Taylor, but he best not disappoint his father when it came to the family business and this Beaumont project. His dad would have no qualms using all the information in the PI's report to his fullest advantage. His dad wanted the puzzle complete and symmetrical, not something looking like a gerrymandered political district. Jack had to find some sort of way to secure Jamestown before his father decided he'd waited long enough and took over the purchasing himself.

Even though his dad was ethical, he was also a tornado when thwarted. He ran over everything in his way by throwing enough money at it. Jack didn't want that for Jayne and Marvin. Sierra wouldn't forgive him. It was up to Jack to create an option that would make all parties happy, but so far a solution had eluded him.

The extra course over, their server removed the place settings. Taylor smiled at him, and Jack knew any other man would be giddy for her attentions. She was a great person—even if she was a little sheltered and snobby—but not a match for him, beyond being his personal assistant. "That was good," she gushed. "I'm so glad you agreed to do this. We've needed an outing, wouldn't you agree?"

He didn't want to be cruel. He'd hoped she'd read his obvious clues. But now he'd have to gently break it to her and send her home. "We were here last weekend."

"Yes, but with you wanting to purchase this place, you should investigate every aspect of the winery. I had my doubts the chef could pull off a menu like this."

He bristled. "Why? Because Beaumont is so small? Provincial? Backwater?"

"Well, no." Taylor leaned back, surprised and a tad off-kilter.

He wished he'd regretted snapping, but her disparaging where he'd grown up slighted each and every person sitting in this room, as well as those working in the back. Strange he felt the need to defend them when he never had before. He tried to catch Sierra's eye, but she kept her head turned.

Taylor ignored his irritation. "Even you have to admit bigger opportunities lie elsewhere. There's more culture, people and action where we live. As for this being a backwater, even you have to admit that the Saks and Neiman Marcus stores in St. Louis only have two floors. Really, that's tiny."

"Retail is moving more and more online. In the end it might turn out to be a wise business decision on their part. Look, here's the next wine pouring."

Thank goodness. He wasn't sure how this night would turn out, but sensed that aside from the food, it wouldn't be good.

Chapter Fifteen

By the end of the fifth course, at least Sierra's stomach was deliriously happy. The delicious filet mignon cooked medium-well had been accompanied by sautéed broccolini and scalloped potatoes. She'd eaten every last bite, earning another membership into the clean plate club. The only thing from keeping her from being completely stuffed was the timing of the courses. To space out the three-and-a-half-hour meal, each new course didn't appear the immediate moment the plates from the previous round disappeared.

Sierra lifted her spoon. Dessert was a sorbet made from a combination of winery grapes and verjus. A chocolate crèmeux—Sierra's favorite—would follow. As always, Jamestown's chef had outdone himself, and the delicious food and wine had mellowed her somewhat. *Somewhat* being rather operative.

She'd done everything in her power to focus on having a great time with her best friend. She'd even had a few minutes to talk to her cousin Andrea and her friend Caleb and hear about the self-service wine bar he'd opened on Main Street. She and Emily had promised to check it out. Sierra had noticed some tension between her cousin and Caleb but hadn't pried. He and Andrea had been best friends forever; she was sure they'd work it out.

The unknown was whether Sierra and Jack could. He remained the elephant in the room. Emily, to her credit, kept the conversation going. She'd always been able to make Sierra laugh, and tonight was no exception. Sierra determined to buy Emily an extra-special Christmas present, along with nominating her for sainthood.

Emily kept insisting she was having a great time—she was thankful to be out of the house and having a girls' night. But Sierra hated that thoughts of Jack kept sneaking in and diverting her attention. Was Jack having a great time with Taylor? Would he take her back to wherever he was staying and make love to her? Even from across the room, Sierra could tell what Taylor wanted. A woman always knew when another woman was after a man. It was evident in the posture. The flirtatious glances. The dip of the chin. The flip of a strand of hair.

The only thing keeping Sierra seated, besides pride and the fact she would embarrass her family, was that Jack didn't appear to be responding. Maybe he didn't need to. Taylor seemed primed no matter what.

Had Sierra been like that Monday night? Had she sent Jack "I'm available" signals? Mortification spread and Sierra grabbed her water goblet. Jack was not her man. He might not have known about the bet, but he was high on her list of failures. Not quite plane crash level, but close enough.

Sierra was an expert at compartmentalizing, but the attractiveness of Jack Clayton made it damn difficult. Fewer than four days between a fantastic orgasm under his ministrations and seeing him on a date with Taylor made forgetting him impossible.

Emily's phone pinged. "Hey, my hubby has a question. Do you mind?"

"Nope. Have to use the restroom anyway." Sierra rose and headed toward the back hallway. She was washing her hands when Taylor entered, and Sierra caught the woman's gaze through the mirror. *Do not engage. Do not engage.*

"You're Sierra, aren't you?" Taylor asked, tone pleasant.

Crap. Engage, but reveal as little as possible. Sierra pumped some soap into her palm. "Yes."

"Your parents own this winery."

What a dumb question. Taylor already knew the

answer. Sierra refrained from glancing heavenward. "Yes."

If Taylor had hoped for a more substantial, less monosyllabic answer, she didn't show it. Her face never changed from being sunny and cheerful. "It was a lovely meal. I was surprised to find something this good in such a rural area. Your chef is excellent."

What a patronizing—Sierra checked the foul word beginning with a *B*. She also checked the "No shit" in defense of the chef. Instead she mimicked the same pleasant tone. "Thank you."

Finished washing her hands, Sierra had to turn Taylor's direction in order to reach the paper towel dispenser. That meant they faced each other in the flesh instead of through the mirror's reflection.

"Has your chef worked here long?" Taylor asked.

Damn it. Sierra would have to answer using more than two words. "He's been here about three years. Said the area reminds him of his native Germany. He studied at CIA." His wife was another reason he was here—a Beaumont native, she'd inherited her family's organic farm, which was where most of the locally grown produce for the dinner had originated.

"CIA," Taylor repeated. "He's a spy?"

Was Taylor that dense? "Culinary Institute of America. One of the top cooking schools in the world."

"Speaking of schools, you went to high school with Jack, right?"

Maybe Taylor was smarter than Sierra had given

her credit for. Nice segue. But Sierra wasn't going to fall for it. "Yes."

"Were you friends?" Taylor was openly fishing and making no effort to hide it.

Sierra really wanted this conversation to end. She had no desire to engage with whatever information-gathering expedition Taylor was on. "I tutored him in math."

Taylor blinked thick long lashes that had to be extensions. "But you're younger than he is, aren't you?"

Sierra couldn't help herself. She smirked. "By two years. I was accelerated. He needed a lot of help to pass algebra."

There. That little dig would serve Jack right for messing with Sierra's head. And, as predicted, Taylor rose to Jack's defense. "He's got an MBA from Stanford."

Time to fully engage and end this. "And I attended the Naval Academy so I could be an aerospace engineer, get my master's, be a lieutenant and fly billion-dollar planes. We are who we are." Patience worn thin, Sierra wadded the paper towels into a ball and tossed them into the waste receptacle in a perfectly made arc. "I need to get back."

"It was nice to meet you. A friend of Jack's should be a friend of mine. Jack and I hit it off right away." Taylor leaned closer, which meant Sierra stepped toward the door. "I'm hoping that working for him and my being here will spur things along. Our parents have plans. They've known each other for years."

Deep down, Sierra knew Taylor's words were probably mostly bluff or an exaggerated wishful thinking, a way to outflank her enemy, but the woman's confidence stung anyway. Taylor was here tonight with Jack, who hadn't even had the decency to text Sierra after spending time loving on her breast. A lifetime of facing down those who doubted her—and who made bets about her—afforded Sierra with impenetrable armor. She would not let Taylor claim this win.

Sierra snorted, something Taylor certainly wasn't expecting as the woman's mouth dropped open with surprise. "Good luck with that," Sierra told her, using a tone holding enough of the unspoken "you're a fool" to make her point. "Jack has a bad habit of making promises he has no intention of keeping. Woman to woman? Don't get suckered by his pretty face. We didn't call him Jerk Clayton in high school for no reason."

After launching that, Sierra stepped past the woman and out the door. She returned to her seat and found the final course waiting. Good thing. She needed chocolate—stat.

"I was about to send out a search party." Concerned eyes offset Emily's joking. "Dessert was here and you weren't. That never happens."

"Taylor and I had a little chat in the bathroom." Sierra filled Emily in. "You should have seen her face when I called him Jerk Clayton. I wonder if she has the guts to tell him."

Emily's right eyebrow arched. "Would you?"

"Probably not. But if you could have seen her expression… That round went to me. Although it feels like a hollow victory." Sierra spooned some of the yummy dessert into her mouth. "If she says anything, I'd expect him to be storm over here. She won't, though, because I'm not a threat. You know what? Forget men. I'm buying a vibrator and calling it Bob. At least it won't disappoint or lie to me."

"At least you know her true intentions, even if he doesn't."

"Of course he does. Their parents want this match so he's probably hedging his bets." Sierra winced at her use of the term. "His choices are girl from the past he might want to sleep with for old time's sake versus the one who his parents love and who wears designer dresses. I'm coveting her outfit. I could never afford that."

They both studied Taylor as she made her way back toward Jack. "That dress is Alexander McQueen," Sierra said. "This season's fashion. I saw it on the Saks app."

"You really need to stop searching that," Emily chided.

"Somehow I got on an email list, so I click through.

The clothes are gorgeous. I wore a uniform for so long, and now that I don't have to, it's fun to dream. What else will I have to spend my Boeing salary on?"

"Rent?"

"Yeah, I'll move out eventually to shorten the hour-long commute. But right now my mom needs my help. Besides, I can dress frugally. Andrea showed me the website she uses where you can rent clothes. That's where she gets half her wardrobe since she can't be seen in the same thing. Influencer stuff or something. I wouldn't know." Sierra had no desire to get on social media.

Emily sipped her wine. "You know what I love about you? You live in the real world. You're the most grounded person I know. Don't change."

"I'm literally grounded if I can't get over my fear of flying." The decadent chocolate dessert lost some of its flavor, and Sierra set down the spoon. "Did I tell you I have an appointment with a new therapist? She had a cancellation next week, so I caught a break to get in early."

"I know this is so difficult for you."

"I'm not going to let the PTSD beat me." Sierra pushed the rest of her dessert forward. "Do you want any of this? If not, I'll take it home."

Emily reached for the plate. "Calories don't count if you're eating out. Gimme. I'll run an extra few miles tomorrow morning, not that it'll make a dent. But oh, so yummy."

"It's all yours. It'll make up for me being a bit of a grump tonight. You've carried the entire evening."

"Not your fault. You didn't know he was coming. He does dominate the space. Look how people are going over and talking to him. He's king of the room."

"Because he's buying everything, they'll court him to see if they can benefit. Too bad I can't ban him from the premises. That would be fun." Sierra glanced around. The event had sold out last weekend, and everyone stayed through dessert. Their server had offered them coffee, but both she and Emily had turned that down. Once dessert ended, guests began leaving as it was a quarter after nine. "You about ready?" Sierra asked.

"Yeah. I have to get home to reality. Hopefully my hubby wrangled the kids into bed. I better not find them awake this late." Emily rose. "My turn to use the bathroom and then we'll go."

"I'll meet you out front." Sierra stood. Guests paid event fees and gratuities when making the reservation, which eliminated checkout. The night weather perfect, Sierra remained under the portico and watched the upper parking lot clear. A few years ago her dad had begun a shuttle service to the lower parking lot, and that bus was in use tonight. Even before his early onset Alzheimer's diagnosis, her dad had ensured the right people were in place to ensure Jamestown's success.

"Sierra."

She'd know that sexy but conniving voice any-where. She tamped down her body's excited re-action—when it came to Jack her libido had no scruples—and gave him a saccharine smile. "Jack. How was your dinner? You and your date looked cozy. She's a great girl. Told me in the bathroom all about how your parents want you to marry her."

"It was dinner, not a date, and there's no chance in hell of me marrying her. Let me explain."

Sierra gave an exaggerated wave, as if brush-ing off a mosquito. "No need and no worries. Tay-lor explained everything while she and I were in the bathroom. She's perfect for you and your so-cial standing."

He winced. "It's not like that."

Sierra shrugged. "It's fine, Jack. Relax. No wor-ries. You and I aren't a thing and what happened wasn't anything either of us needs to write home about. We got carried away, that was all. A little fairy dust. Some elfin magic making us act out of sorts. Maybe curiosity. It's not like it meant anything."

Jack growled low and hard. "Don't you dare dis-count things."

Sierra's hands went to her hips and she puckered her lips. "Don't you dare blow them out of propor-tion. Ah, here's Emily. Emily, you remember Jack."

"Jack. I'd say it's good to see you but you know that's not the case." Sierra tried not to snicker at

Emily's frosty tone. "Did you leave your date at the table? That's rather rude, isn't it?"

Even beaten, Jack didn't give up. "She's my PA and I wanted to talk to Sierra. Sierra, listen, I—"

Sierra cut him off with a stop motion of her hand. "I don't want to hear it. I'll contact you when we need to chat about the Halloween festival. We're still stuck with that, I suppose. I'm sure we can manage to tolerate each other Saturday and get the job done."

With that, she and Emily stepped off the sidewalk and headed toward Sierra's car. "Good job," Emily said. "You handled that superbly."

"I'm not sure if I feel good about acting like a bitch, but I did hold my ground," Sierra replied. "That was the thing to do, right?"

Emily nodded. "You showed him you're not a pushover and that he's not going to walk all over you again. Do not turn around to see if he's still standing there. He's not. He went inside."

Sierra had been about to turn. She pressed her key fob and the interior lights brightened as the car unlocked. "I had more courage tonight than I did in high school. That part felt great."

"The military was good for something."

"Many things actually," Sierra corrected. She reached for the Breathalyzer she'd bought after watching Jack use his. She was under the limit and safe to drive. "He came after me, you saw that."

Emily's voice held warning. "Don't read anything into it. Not this time. Don't you dare fall for the man again unless you're sure he's not using you."

Sierra wavered. She blamed it on her hormones. "I told you he didn't know about the bet."

"Whatever. That's irrelevant now. I'm supportive of you giving him payback. Of making him work the Halloween festival. I'll actually concede some and say you can use him for sex as long as you don't pour your heart out. In fact, if you broke his heart, I'd be happy. He'd deserve it. I don't like seeing you hurt and that's all he's ever done. You have things to accomplish."

Emily meant Sierra's PTSD. "Despite what I might say, I'm not the kind to sleep around."

Emily nodded. "Which is why your heart is already too involved if you kissed him like you told me you did Monday night. You've always had a thing for him. Maybe you should sleep with him and get him out of your system. Maybe the sex won't be everything you fantasized and you can finally let the fantasy go. I don't know if that's the correct choice, but I'll support you in anything you do. Even if I have to help you pick up the pieces again."

Sierra started the car and drove slowly from the parking lot, watching for other diners who might be leaving. "Would that really work?" she asked Emily. "Or would it be like getting a box of chocolates? Or a bag of chips? Or delicious cookies? You think you'll eat one, but by the time you're able to stop, you realize you've eaten half the box."

"The good thing is you don't have to decide what to do tonight. Go home. Sleep on it. Alone." Emily's phone pinged. She sighed. "Jeff's having difficulty with one of the twins."

"Tell you what, I'll come babysit one afternoon and you can go rent a room for an hour or so and have some me time with your hubby. You can leave the twins with me. I'll do godmother duty."

Fingers tapping, Emily sighed. "Don't joke. That sounds heavenly."

Sierra watched for deer as she drove on Winery Road toward historic Beaumont. Emily and Jeff lived in Emily's childhood home, a mansion situated one block west of Main Street. The 1890s homestead, purchased in the 1910s and passed down through the generations, symbolized her family's success as one of the first Black families to settle in Beaumont and build a thriving business. When she reached Emily's house, lights blazed from every window, even the third floor. Jeff appeared in the doorway, the porch light shining on his white and haggard skin.

"I'm serious about the babysitting. You and Jeff can have wild, no-holds-barred sex," Sierra said.

Emily half laughed, half sighed as she climbed out of the car. "Oh, Sierra, you have so much to learn. If Jeff and I got a room, even for an hour, both of us would use it to sleep. Talk soon. And I'm taking you up on that sitter offer. Sleep sounds lovely."

Sierra leaned on the steering wheel so she could see Emily through the open passenger door. She waved at Jeff. "Do. Thanks for being my bestie."

"Anytime. Love ya like a sister."

Sierra waited until Emily was inside before driving off. She drove slowly up the gravel drive, her headlights landing on the darkened house. Her mom and dad must already be asleep. She began to turn the wheel and stopped. A Mercedes convertible was parked next to her spot. She pulled in, and Jack uncurled from the front seat.

Because her parents were asleep, she shut the car door softly and with less than normal force. Her voice, however, came out strong and snappy. "Why are you here?"

"Because we need to talk."

Tingles began and Sierra fought them. "We have nothing to discuss. Where's Taylor?"

"I dropped her at the B&B."

Sierra's sarcasm echoed in the night. "I'm sure she loved that."

Jack scowled. "I don't care what she loves. She and I are not dating, and I made that clear on the drive home."

An owl hooted in the distance. "Did she cry when you told her?"

Jack's expression morphed into confusion. "What? No. Why would she do that?"

Men were so clueless. "If she didn't cry, then she doesn't believe you. Heck, I don't believe you. She's perfect. Blonde. Pretty. Dresses well. Just what the parents ordered."

Jack raked his hand through his hair. "I do not do what my parents want all the time."

"Uh-huh." Her disbelieving tone carried softly and clearly.

"Look, I know I messed up. I'm sorry I didn't call or text. I had to fly to Portland last minute. I left hours after I left you. Then I was in nonstop meetings, and to make matters worse, my phone got wet in a freak accident when I dropped it in a puddle and I had to replace it and download everything from the cloud."

Of course Jack was the type of guy who simply bought a new phone.

"I was wrong to ghost you," he continued. "I had a lot I had to deal with in a short period of time. My dad—it doesn't matter. You were never far from my thoughts. I'm sorry."

She couldn't let his earnestness sway her. "You seem to be sorry a lot where I'm concerned. I don't think this is a good idea." She circled her forefinger for emphasis. "Whatever this sexual attraction is between us, it's most likely hormones. Pheromones. Nostalgia. Something. We might be attracted to each other, but we come from different worlds and live in different places. Taylor and her Alexander McQueen dress made that clear."

His hair stood up where he'd jerked his hand through it. "What does her dress have anything to do with it? Who's Alexander McQueen?"

"The fact you don't understand that shows why we have nothing in common. It's a high-end designer brand."

"Why should I care about that? I don't understand what you're trying to get at. I could not care less about what label you wear." Clearly frustrated, Jack kicked some gravel with his toe. "I want to get to know you. I'd like you if you were wearing a potato sack."

"That's a cliché and no, you wouldn't. You want my land, not me."

"My dad wants your land and it's my job to get it. There's a big difference."

"No, it's the same thing," Sierra shot back. Whatever type of woman he'd marry would be one who knew how to fit into his world. His wife would hold dinner parties with valets and caterers and understand how to manage it all. Sierra knew nothing about those things. Give her an engine, sure, but social stuff? Hell no. While she'd attended military balls and wine dinners, someone else organized them.

"It's totally different," Jack persisted. "Don't

even try to tell me otherwise because you're wrong. Who I am has nothing to do with how much money my parents have."

"Yeah, you've told yourself that enough times so that you believe it. But you're wrong. It has everything to do with why we cannot be together."

"You are the most infuriating woman I know," he bit out. "We can—"

A loud thump sounded in the garage behind them, and both Jack and Sierra froze. They stared at each other as they heard a second thump. Sierra moved, heading to the garage's side entry. The dusk-to-dawn light revealed the door was shut tight. Another thump came from inside.

"What do you think's making that noise?" Jack asked. He was right behind her.

"I don't know. Maybe an animal. That would be the last thing we'd need, a raccoon eating the leather seats of my dad's cars." Sierra keyed in the number to the side door lock. When she stepped inside the darkened space of her dad's garage, the alarm system mounted next to her on the wall didn't beep the way it should. "Someone disarmed this."

She and Jack both heard another thump and the shuffling sound of footsteps. Without thinking of the consequences or of potential dangers, Sierra flipped a switch. Overhead lights flooded the space, making everyone blink. Her dad stood next to his beloved Corvette with the driver's side door open.

He squinted again as if the lights still blinded him. "Who goes there?" her dad called.

Sierra's relief he wasn't an intruder quickly became replaced with concern. "Dad? It's Sierra. What are you doing out here? Why are you in your pajamas? Where are your shoes?"

Her dad leaned over to rummage on the driver's floorboard. "I'm taking my car out for a moonlight spin, but I can't find the thing that starts it."

He was having one of his episodes. "Keys," Sierra said patiently. "You want the keys."

Irritated with her answer, he grew more impatient. "Yes, that's it. Keys. Where are the damn keys? They should be under the seat. That's where I leave them for customers."

Keys for all the classic cars in his garage were locked up in a fireproof safe inside the house. Not that her dad could drive anymore. He couldn't even remember a key was a key. "Why aren't my keys here? I have to make sure the bodywork I did is perfect. That requires a test drive."

Before she could stop herself, Sierra burst into tears. She wiped her face furiously, and eye shadow and mascara smeared onto her red silk cuffs. She refused to cry more, especially in front of Jack.

Recognizing her discomfort, Jack moved around her.

"Mr. James. It's me, Jack Clayton. I've got a Mercedes convertible outside."

"Jack? Are you a new client? Do you need body-work? It's late and I'm about to close. You'll have to come back tomorrow and I'll see when I can fit you in. But you say a Mercedes? That's a nice car."

"No, I don't need any bodywork. But I could use your help. How about you let me take you for a drive and let you see what the car can do? We'll put the top down. The night's nice enough for that, especially if Sierra gets you a jacket." And shoes, Jack mouthed back at her.

"So is it a '58 220 Cabriolet? Worked once on a four-speed, inline six. Sweet ride. Tell you what, I'll fit you in since you seem like a nice guy. A Mer-cedes, you say."

Sierra ground her knuckles into her mouth to keep from sobbing. Her father, always a pillar of strength, now lived in his own world that took him away from everyone and everything he'd loved.

With infinite patience, Jack shut the door to the Corvette and began to guide her father from the ga-rage. "This one's a little newer than '58. Let's see if you like it."

Sierra set the alarm, locked the door and followed the two men. She skirted around them and took the porch steps two at a time. As she entered the kitchen, her mom came rushing down the stairs, her hair topsy-turvy and her bathrobe flapping behind her.

"Dad's okay. He's outside with Jack," Sierra re-assured her.

"Thank goodness. I woke up and he wasn't there." Wide-eyed, her mom headed for the back door. "He's never done this."

"He was in the garage looking for his keys. He wanted to go for a drive. Jack told him he'd take him. That's where he is now."

Sierra's mom pulled on a housecoat and grabbed a jacket for her husband. Carrying a pair of her dad's slip-on shoes, Sierra followed her outside. "Marvin," her mom called.

He waved at her. "Hey, Jayne. Was going to take you for a moonlight drive but then this nice man said he needed help with his car. It's a sweet ride. Look at those wheels, Jayne. You ever seen 'em look like that?"

Her mom's shoulders sagged with relief at the recognition. She and Sierra approached Jack's car, which had the hood up and the top down. Her dad listened as Jack explained the engine. "Those are a lot of horses," her dad said. "Let's go see what they can do."

"How about you two go on ahead? Sierra and I can sit out on the porch while you and Jack talk cars." Sierra's mom made her voice chipper and bright, but Sierra heard the underlying strain.

Sierra's dad pointed to the engine block. "He's been telling me about the engine. Even showed me a short video. Look at these modern things. Don't look like they used to."

"No, they certainly don't," Sierra's mom agreed. She dressed her husband in his coat and shoes and returned to the porch, where she sank into one of the white rocking chairs. Sierra took the one beside her. They rocked back and forth and watched as Jack checked on her father's seat belt. The car roared to life.

"We won't be long," Jack yelled over the din. Then he slowly drove down the driveway, and Sierra could hear her dad whooping with glee.

"You okay?" she asked her mom.

"Honestly? No." Her mom rose, went into the house and, with shaking hands, filled a teakettle. "I panicked. He's losing more and more memory. I didn't ever expect to wake up and find him gone."

"Jack'll drive him around. He'll like that."

"He's a good one, that boy. I know you've had your differences, but not many men of his caliber would have the type of patience needed to deal with your father. He's a keeper."

"He's not my man, Mom." And he never would be.

Still, Sierra had to give Jack credit where credit was due. "It's hard to know who he really is. He wants our winery. He might be willing to be patient with dad just to get what he wants. I don't know what his intentions are. I don't trust him."

"Honey, we've had so many offers over the years"

"Why haven't you told me?"

"Because it's nothing I can't handle, and back to that boy, I can't believe he's all bad. Not from the way he looks at you. He can't fake his feelings." Her mom sighed. "I don't know exactly what happened between you in high school, but that was a long time ago. It's about what's inside a person that matters. You'll figure it out. You have a good head on your shoulders."

Sierra wasn't certain what was inside Jack. Was it integrity? She had no idea what made him tick, minus buying wineries and making tons of money. But seeing him care for her dad had diffused her earlier anger. Family came first, and Jack's actions of doing the right thing, without any prompting, spoke volumes. He'd simply stepped up and filled a need. Even if he mentioned buying the winery while out on the drive, her dad wouldn't remember. Nothing her dad would say could be binding.

Her heart was already far too involved. Sierra felt like a tennis ball being banged around in a championship match. Jack was more than her kryptonite. He was a tractor beam drawing her to the Death Star. Worse, she wanted to give in to the pull.

The teakettle whistled, and her mom lifted it from the stove. Pouring, her mom began to seep two cups containing lemon and ginger tea bags. "Drink this. It'll help."

"Thanks." Sierra bobbed the bag repeatedly, watching as the water turned a translucent yellow.

Removing the bag, she set it on a small plate before she added a small amount of honey to the brew. She'd never been one who added milk. When the tea had cooled slightly, she sipped. "This is good."

"It's a new blend from the tea shop on Main Street." Her mom held the cup to her lips and drank deeply. "It's become a very popular place. You should check it out next time you're in town. Take a break and walk down there."

"I will." Sierra sipped, her mind racing. How could her mom be so giving and calm? Jayne was a pillar of strength, with reserve for her daughter. Sierra never would have predicted the night to have turned out like this. "Do you think they'll be back soon?"

Her mom appeared a picture of calm, not worried that her husband was out for a joyride with the enemy. "It'll take as long as it takes. Your dad is enjoying himself. Let him enjoy the thrill of a powerful vehicle. It's not like he gets that in the SUV when I take him to his adult day camp."

"I'm sorry I wasn't around to help when this all started."

Her mom shook her head. "Don't be. It's not your fault or your responsibility. You girls need to live your lives. He'd hate it if he knew you were putting your plans on hold for him. That would be the last thing he'd want. It's why we didn't tell either of you right away. He didn't want to make you feel you had to choose when there's nothing you can do."

Sierra drank deeply. Then she took the spoon and stirred several more times. "I've got an appointment with a new therapist and I accepted the offer with Boeing. It's time for me to get my life together. I'll work with other pilots. The project's classified or I'd tell you about it. But when I was there a while ago, they all called each other by their pilot names."

"It's a fabulous opportunity. You deserve it."

"It means I won't be around as much to help with the winery or cookie store. I'll be full time."

Her mom patted her hand. "But engineering is where your heart is. If you can't be flying for the navy, you can help others soar. I know you want to be involved, but caring for your father is not your or your sister's job. It's mine. I married your dad for better or for worse, and he and I will make decisions together. We will keep you and your sister informed, but this is our life as a married couple."

"But some days he doesn't know who we are." Sierra's stomach churned, the night's delicious dinner making its presence known the more anxious she became.

"And other days he does. Even when he doesn't know me, deep in his heart he does. He writes me love letters. He knows I'm someone who matters to him, even if his brain wiring means he can't remember my name."

Sierra hadn't realized how bad her dad's condition had gotten. "That has to be so hard on you."

Her mom patted her hand again. "It is, which is why I've got my own therapist to speak with. So don't worry about me. Well, I know you'll worry, so be assured I'm on top of things. The thing I want most for you girls is your happiness. I can't be worrying about both of you at the same time I'm worrying about him."

"Okay. That's fair. You tell me if I can do more. Name it. I'll help. And I'll try harder so you don't have to worry about me. I'm going to be okay."

"Thank you. And I know you are. You've got a will of iron. You're strong. You will get through this and be happy. I know it here." Her mom pressed a fist to her heart. Then she pointed. "That's them now."

The low rumble of an engine mixed with the crunch of gravel. Sierra followed her mom onto the porch. Jack parked the car, and her dad got out. "Woo, Jaynie! That car sure flies. You should go for a spin."

Her mom gave him a huge smile that broke Sierra's heart. "What a great idea. But not tonight. Maybe tomorrow. Jack needs to go home, and it's past your bedtime."

Her dad fingered his shirttail. "Is that why I'm in my pajamas?"

Her mom gave a quick nod. "Yes. Say thanks to Jack for the adventure and let's go inside. I'm tired."

"Thanks, Jack." Her dad shook Jack's hand before following his wife inside. Sierra remained rooted on the porch. Jack climbed the stairs. He put one foot near hers, but kept the other on the lower steps. He lightly held on to the stair railing.

"You still mad at me?" he asked.

She shook her head. "No. How can I be angry when you're so kind to my father? But that doesn't mean I'm happy or that I forgive you."

He gave her a lopsided grin. "Didn't think I'd get out of the doghouse that easily. Believe me, I realize why you've put me in there and I'll do what it takes to get out."

"Still won't change the fact we're ill-suited," Sierra said. "This won't work."

"Let me prove you wrong. I'll let you drive my car to make you like me."

She appreciated his attempt at humor. "Unlike my dad, I don't find your car a temptation." He was, but she'd exercise self-control, no matter how tenuous. She really wanted to hug him and take comfort in his arms, but that might lead somewhere her head wasn't ready to go.

Her mom appeared in the doorway. "I'm going back to bed. Your dad's already asleep."

Sierra's eyes widened in surprise. "That was fast."

Her mom's smile held sadness. "He wore himself out. He doesn't have the energy he once had."

"Do any of us?" Jack's quip lightened the moment. "He talked the entire way. He loved the car. I enjoyed giving him a ride."

"Cars are his favorite things and often what he clings to the most. Thank you for taking him. I know it's late, but if you and Sierra wanted to talk, you could sit out on the gazebo or in the fairy garden. Don't leave on my account."

Sierra nixed that idea. "I'll be right in. We're saying goodbye now."

"I do have to go," Jack agreed. "It was good to see you, Mrs. James."

"Feel free to come around more often. You're always welcome." Her mom closed the kitchen door behind her, disappearing from view.

Jack stepped to the ground. "As much as I'd like to revisit the fairy garden with you, I meant it when I said I should leave. I like you, and I don't want us muddling things any more tonight by adding the physical. How about I see you tomorrow? Maybe dinner?"

"I'm working tomorrow for my sister and have an appointment after that. I'll see you at the festival planning Saturday. I'll meet you there. Fair?"

"Yes." He turned away first, climbing into the driver's seat. He pointed the car toward the county road and shifted into Drive. As he headed down the driveway, the rising dust created a low foggy mist. A pang went through her. His leaving was what she wanted, right?

Then why were her fingers itching to caress his jawline? Maybe plant kisses down it? Why did her heart feel as if it was shredding from inside out? Why was it they'd been off to the races a few days ago and now were stopped in the tracks? Why couldn't she rationalize away the mental? Just have a physical fling? Not worry whom else he might be with? Trust and believe he wasn't with Taylor and wanted her instead? Why did something so wrong seem oh so right?

He'd captured her attention and taken up residence in her head. She had no idea what was up or down, like a plane lost in the blue of the horizon without an altimeter to right itself. She'd lost sight of her game plan, her strategy, with no clue what she was even fighting for, or against. He was making her lose her mind. People crashed and burned that way, the last thing she needed. She'd been there, done that. She couldn't risk losing her heart to Jack.

She had enough of a recovery ahead already.

Chapter Sixteen

It seemed half the town showed up for Saturday's Halloween festival meeting, minus Sierra's sister, Zoe, who was home with her sick daughter. Megan had gone home sick Friday, and Zoe had also taken Lacey, the daughter of the school principal, home with her. Sierra knew Zoe liked Jared Dempsey, but her sister was once bitten twice shy. Still, there was something happening between them and Sierra hoped it would work out.

She didn't have the same confidence in her and Jack. The festival planning turned out to be way less about pen-and-paper organization and more about event prep. Along with Jack, she'd been suckered into decorating. However, she was inside and he was out.

If all went well, around mid-Saturday next weekend, the committee's efforts would see children and families enjoy a corn maze, have their faces painted and play spooky-themed games for candy and small prizes. Luke and Shelby Thornburg, who piloted the hot-air balloon called Playgroup, would stand up their balloon and offer one lucky raffle winner a short ride. Cooks would serve dinner chuck wagon style, and at night Ingersoll's barn would become a dance hall and saloon.

Sierra found herself on decorating duty, in charge of wrapping orange and black streamers around the lower half of each of the four two-story-high support beams. She'd seen Jack briefly, but then he'd disappeared outside with Randy. She hoped he didn't do anything foolish, like hurt Randy. Even if Randy deserved it.

Yesterday afternoon, she'd mentioned Jack to her new therapist, but with the focus on her PTSD from the crash, one session hadn't been enough to delve into her conflicting feelings where Jack was concerned.

While she worked, she kept a look out for him, her heart giving a tiny leap whenever she thought she saw him. He had that easy grin that sucked a woman in and dimples to die for. And how he'd treated her father? He'd won her over. Would sleeping with him get him out of her system? Or would he further embed himself into her heart and life? Get even further under her skin?

Sierra finished wrapping the crepe paper, running out of the black before the orange. She taped the streamers down, straightened and bumped into Paula.

"Good, you're done." Paula held a clipboard and made a check mark on a list Sierra couldn't read upside down. "I can't believe it, but we're almost finished."

Sierra glanced around, noting the decorating scheme was clearly small-town rom-com movie. Hay bales lined the perimeter, stacked to create places to sit. Interlocking wooden planks formed a dance floor. Strings of white and orange fairy lights provided a subtle glow, creating atmosphere. There were designated areas for the DJ and for refreshments.

"All that we need is the food and music and we'll be good to go." Paula made another mark with her pencil. "You're coming, right?"

Sierra's chest tightened. "All I agreed to was to help out. Besides, I haven't owned a Halloween costume in years."

Paula looked up and frowned. "Throw on a tight black top, leggings and some cat ears if you don't coordinate with Jack."

Sierra managed not to drop the roll of tape. "Why would we do that?"

"Because you're a couple. Seriously Sierra, don't be difficult." Paula leaned closer, as if that would help Sierra understand. "Jack likes you and you never did have your dance."

Panic clawed at Sierra's nerves. She'd wanted Jack badly long ago. She couldn't allow him to take her to the town dance. What would everyone think? Would there be bets, like before? The huge barn became claustrophobic. "We're friends. That's all. We were pulling your leg because Randy automatically assumed. Don't make it anything more. Please excuse me. I need to put this tape back in case anyone else needs it."

Sierra headed for the open barn doors that led outside to a sunny, pleasant fall day. In a clearing a distance away, Shelby and Luke inflated Playgroup. The two had been high school sweethearts who hadn't seen each other for ten years before reconnecting. Now they were married. Curious, Sierra edged closer. Luke checked the ropes. Shelby connected the lines. The balloon lay flat on the ground until Luke turned on a huge fan. As soon as enough air blew in and filled the envelope, Shelby fired the burners.

Moments later, the balloon stood straight, its colorful crown pointed to the sky. Sierra didn't realize how close she was until the heat from the firing burners blasted over her. Immediately her skin prickled. Sweat broke out on her forehead, same as the other onlookers. They wore expressions of joy and excitement. Sierra paled and experienced an uncontrollable panic as Playgroup fought her holders to reach the sky. Once upon a time Sierra had loved ballooning. Today she panicked.

Eager bystanders leaned on all four sides of the basket, keeping it grounded. Across the way, Jack's biceps bulged as he helped hold the balloon. Whatever he mouthed at Sierra was lost in the whooshing sound of the burners. She trembled as the scene in front of her swayed, same as the basket that fought to fly. Ears pounding a rapid thumping, Sierra stepped back as images threatened to crowd her mind. She speed-walked back into the barn and grabbed her purse and her windbreaker.

"Sierra, are you okay? You look like you've seen a ghost." Clipboard still in hand, Paula narrowed her gaze and peered at her with concern.

"I'm fine. Just have to go. Sorry I can't help more." Sierra spun on her heel and fought the urge to sprint. Bad enough her heart pounded and her breath gasped short and shallow. She might not be able to control having a panic attack, but she would not have it in front of half the town.

Playgroup was ascending into the sky when Sierra slid inside her car. She reached to close the door and connected with a denim-clad leg. "Hey," Jack said. He held her door open. "Where are you going?"

She had no idea. Hadn't thought beyond getting away. "Anywhere but here."

"I'll take you. Do you trust me?"

She managed a nod, so he helped her from the car before she could refuse. He settled her into the Mercedes passenger seat. The car spun gravel as they left. Sierra stared aimlessly out the window until Jack parked in the lot located behind the former River Bend B&B. She frowned. "This place is closed."

"Yeah, it is. It's our Beaumont headquarters. When we're done we'll renovate and reopen. Come on. Everyone else is back in Portland for the weekend so it'll be quiet." Jack unlocked the back door and keyed in an alarm code. "This way."

He led her through the kitchen and into a wide entry hall that ran the entire width of the house from front to back. Sierra saw that the dining room had been converted into a conference room. The living room contained multiple desks and a huge satellite map hanging on the wall. She went over to the map. "What's this?"

"All of what we own. And what we don't."

Sierra found her family's vineyard—the only significant white space left on the map. No wonder why he wanted her land. From an aerial view, her family's acreage sat dead center.

Jack held out his arm and waved her from the room. "Come on, no business. Follow me." He began ascending the stairs, and Sierra hesitated. "The sitting room is on the second floor," he called. "What, did you think I was taking you to my bedroom?"

Part of her wanted nothing more, to let herself lose herself and forget reality. "How was I to know? I've never been in this place." She reached a large, comfortable landing at the top of the stairs. Two hallways branched off, leading to the guest rooms. Many of the doors stood open, but four remained closed, and Sierra surmised those belonged to Jack, Taylor and the two men she'd seen with him that Sunday.

Jack went to a tiny minifridge and retrieved two bottles of water. He handed her one and gestured to a loveseat. "Sit and tell me what's wrong."

She remained standing. "Nothing. I'm fine now."

"I saw you. You turned sheet white." He patted the cushions.

"I…" Telling him he'd witnessed one of her severe panic attacks made her vulnerable. "You'll use it against me." She knew she sounded irrational but didn't care.

"Sierra."

She liked how her name rolled off his tongue, even when delivered in a patient, "I know you're deflecting" tone. "Jack."

"You still don't get it, do you?" His voice became a low growl. "I care about you. I want to help. To be with you."

"Maybe you're not all bad." Really, no one who

took her dad for a drive could be a terrible person. She awarded him credit. "But knowledge is always power."

"I read about your accident." He winced. "It came up in the report. I'm sorry."

"I don't want your pity." Sierra bristled. Of course he'd have had her family investigated. He had a goal to achieve. Wasn't that why she'd agreed to go with him that Monday, to figure him out?

She should throw a fit and storm out but she was too exhausted. Panic attacks always sucked away her strength. If she were in his position, she'd have done the same thing. Had, sort of. But, because she wasn't in his position of building real estate conglomerates, his investigation of her made the differences between them even starker. She didn't belong in his world. No matter how much chemistry—and currently it flowed between them like a pulsating wave—they didn't have common ground, or that sameness in thought and temperament that allowed a couple to bond. Like Emily and Jeff. Or Sierra's parents.

She and Jack were oil and water, with an attraction rationalized by science. They could mix but that didn't equate to staying power. Like Halley's Comet, he'd come into her orbit and would soon exit, off to buy more properties and build his empire. She should give in to her urges. Experience the sex he offered with no strings and no expectations. The trouble was, she might like being with him. Her heart was already too bruised to risk such foolishness.

"Sierra, come on. Tell me what's going on." Jack gently removed the empty bottle of water from her taut fingertips.

"PTSD. I have PTSD. Did your report tell you that?"

"No." His tone gentled. "I didn't know."

"Well, I have PTSD." Saying the words aloud helped her own the condition, but acknowledging her affliction didn't make the problem disappear. Hopefully her new therapist would continue to help with that. "Being around anything that flies gives me a panic attack, and if it flies and there's also heat and flame…" There, her secret was out. She caught her breath. "You can hold my fears against me. I do."

She waited for his response. Most didn't know what to say besides an awkwardly condescending "I'm sorry." Others gave her unsolicited and un- wanted advice or useless platitudes of "You'll get through it."

Jack set down both of their water bottles. He wrapped his hands around hers. "One thing that's always impressed me is how strong you are. You're fierce. A fighter. You had to be to skip two grades in math and deal with all the assholes, me included. You're a warrior. If you need me, I'm here." He gave her hand a reassuring squeeze.

Sierra fought the delightful shivers. How dare he say something so perfect? How dare he be her dream man? Something always ruined her dreams. They crashed. Burned. Then she rose from the ashes to rebuild like a failed phoenix. She would not let herself fall in love. Could she split herself into two, take the physical release and leave the mental anguish? She'd had enough practice of late doing that with the panic attacks. Could she love Jack with her body while still protecting her mind and heart?

Pilots learned how to set aside emotions and think logically. Currently she enjoyed his delicious thumb stroking the inside of her wrist. If she let go, she could embrace the tingles shooting through her, the very ones turning her knees into jelly and her veins into liquid gold.

As long as she didn't fall in love, she should be fine. She might not be able to control her panic attacks or PTSD, but daily she relied on the mantra that she could control the things she could control.

She freed her hands, put them on each side of his face and brought her lips to his. He quickly recovered from his shock, kissing her back with a ferocity that left no doubt to his desire and intentions. "Sierra," he groaned as she ran her lips along his jawline.

"Let me be in control," she urged, and as she pushed his chest, Jack reclined against the back of the plush loveseat. She straddled the tops of his thighs and ran kisses over his throat and down to the hollow. She pressed her lips against his collarbone and began working on undoing the buttons of his shirt. When he started to say something, she captured his lips and found his tongue with hers.

After she kissed him long and hard, she stripped him of his clothes. She took him into her mouth, fulfilling her fantasy as his hands stroked her hair. "Damn that's good," he said. "Sierra…"

But he could say no more as Sierra worked her magic. Perhaps she'd started making love as a way to prove she had some control over this at least. But with Jack the act turned into something beyond foreplay. She felt him shift. "Sierra, I'm…"

Too bad. She wanted him out of control. Weak to her power. She worked until she left him limp and spent.

As she rose to her feet, Jack recovered and stood before she did. "Where do you think you're going?"

She'd been about to say *home*, but her car was at Ingersoll's. He didn't wait for her reply anyway, sweeping her into his arms. He nudged open one of the hall doors and laid her down on a huge, four-poster bed. Vaguely, she noted the Victorian decor as Jack began removing her clothes. He was impressive, and she drank him in. "I promised myself that night in the fairy garden I was going to make you come again."

"You did?"

"I did and I am."

He'd also said their first time should not be on a forest floor, and here they were in a queen-size bed. Sierra crooked her forefinger and he kissed her senseless until he went back to removing her clothing. He dropped her jeans to the floor and she lay spread out. His forefinger circled the source of her pleasure. She bucked. "You are beautiful."

"I—I b-bet you say that to all the g-girls." She gasped out the words as he made her tremble.

"Not even close." Tone serious, he pressed a finger into her, eliciting a needy whimper. She reached for him, but he sidestepped. "You like control, huh? Let's see you lose it for once. How does that sound? Fair's fair, right? It's your turn again."

"F-fine," Sierra conceded as he bent to bring his mouth to her core. "H-have it your way. Oh!" As if held in reserve from their last time together under the strands of fairy lights, her legs trembled as wave after wave of pleasure washed over her.

He climbed onto the bed and started driving her wild. Enough of this, Sierra thought, wrapping her legs around him. With one push of her elbows into the firm mattress to add some leverage, she rolled him over on his back and took control again, including protecting them both.

Wickedness etched her smile as she finally claimed him as hers. "Witch," he hissed, his eyes closing momentarily.

"Don't you forget it." Already every pore clamored with passionate sensations. Craving him made her quiver, the sex one hundred times better than her one and only previous lover. She was ready, willing and open. The heat fused their bodies and musk scented the air. Already she could tell that this would be the orgasm to end all orgasms.

"That's it," he encouraged. "Take me."

"I will," she told him, letting the pressure build. Her body shook. She soared. She flew, any insecurities replaced with scintillating sensations until his energy provided her with one last propulsion that sent her splintering into dozens of delicious lights. Spent, she slowly floated down from the high.

Without breaking their union, Jack rolled her to her side and wrapped himself around her. He drew her into his arms and kissed her neck. If she never moved again, she wouldn't mind. Who knew sex could be as great as hurtling through the sky in a T-6? She could stay like this forever.

But it was midafternoon. She shifted, and Jack pulled her tighter. "Later can wait," he said, his breath heated against her neck. "Stay."

Should she? Her languid, lazy and well-loved body didn't want to leave. Her forward-thinking brain warned that pilots who flew beyond the limits risked running out of fuel. "For a little while longer," she compromised, caving to the delicious tingles he created as he kissed behind her ear.

Long ago, she'd wanted Jack to be the one. Had fantasized about being in his arms just like this. While that dream had died like so many others, she could allow herself this long afternoon to pretend things had turned out differently. She could give herself over to an incredible lover whose fingers were already creating new magic. In sex, her body and mind weren't broken or suffering. They functioned perfectly together, as normally as she had once controlled her fighter jet.

She refused to contemplate why sex had never been this good before. Then his mouth found her breast, making all rationalizations disappear as she whimpered her pleasure. Her fingers threaded into silken hair. Her back arched. As another orgasm began to sweep through her, Sierra let go.

When Sierra next opened her eyes, dark shadows covered the room like sheets over furniture in a house closed for the season. Her watch told her it was nearing seven. A growl of her stomach indicated it had been hours since she'd eaten. Beside her, Jack slept on his back, one arm crooked over his eyes. His other hand rested loosely against her left thigh.

Time to leave. She couldn't spend the night, even though her body would be happy never moving again. She shifted, easing slowly as not to wake him. Moving quickly, she performed the required task of locating and donning her clothes. She made it all the way down the stairs without a creak and darted into the half bath beneath the stairs.

When she opened the door, she found Jack standing there wearing nothing but plaid boxers. She stopped short.

"Planning on leaving without saying goodbye?" His leashed anger and recrimination sent both thrills and chills over her.

She played it nonchalantly. "Figured it'd be easier."

He arched an eyebrow. "With your car sitting at Ingersoll's? Planning on swiping my Mercedes?"

"Well, it's one way I'd get to drive it." She shrugged. "Besides, you can afford an Uber if I do. Plenty of those around for an hour or so after the wineries close."

"Whether or not I can afford an Uber is irrelevant. The real question is why you're sneaking out like a thief. Are you ashamed of what we did?" One hand planted on his right hip.

Was she? "I was trying to avoid that awkward conversation we now seem to be having," Sierra defended.

Jack exhaled frustration and gestured. "Why should it be awkward? Unless you regret it. Do you? For I sure don't. Damn, Sierra, you're a hard one to figure out but I'm trying."

She bristled. "Don't turn this around on me."

His expression softened. "That's not my intention. I'm explaining that I'm finding it impossible
to get close to you."

"We were as close as two people can be," Sierra
argued.

"Besides that!" Jack calmed himself before try-
ing again. "You push me away at every opportunity.
I don't want a one-night stand. I want you, Sierra.
All of you. I always have."

She didn't believe him. "You told me casual sex."

His hair stood straight after he raked his fingers
through it. "No, those were your words. If I'd only
wanted sex, I had Taylor living under my roof. I
don't want her and I've not touched her. In fact, I
sent her back to Portland for good."

"You did?" Hope bubbled like a busy brook, but
Sierra ignored the sensation. The word *hopeful* was
too close to *hope fell*. Or *hope hell*.

"I don't want her as anything but an assistant and
it's not fair to her to keep her in Beaumont when
she hates it here. I offered her a nice severance and
sent her packing. My office manager will source
her replacement. You'll like Doris. She's sixty and
happily married. She already loves you. Says any
woman who has me this knotted must be great."

Sierra shook her head to clear away the relief.
She couldn't let herself get swept away as she had
this afternoon. "This is overwhelming. I can't com-
plicate things."

"Why is our being together overwhelming? Give me one good reason why what we've shared is complicated besides my wanting your parents' winery."

Because her heart still wanted him. Because she didn't even know fully who she was anymore until she sorted out the PTSD. She'd lost her naval career because of panic attacks she still couldn't control. Who was she without it? The scary part was figuring that out. She couldn't confuse great sex for something more. The fallout would be terrible. "It's like I'm sleeping with the enemy. That's enough of a complication."

"I am not sleeping with you to get a winery." He practically growled out the words. "I want you because when you're in my arms it feels like I'm touching heaven. When I'm inside you it's better than anything else and I lose myself. Sex aside, I crave your mind. It challenges mine. Case in point, this moment. Damn, I want all of you, Sierra. Something beyond lust. It's why I asked you to homecoming even though I was moving. Because we had no future then, I let myself be greedy. I wanted one date with you that I could carry with me forever."

She couldn't let his declaration sway her. She was nothing if not practical. "We still have no future. And you just got your night."

He stepped toward her. "I want another. Then another. I want to date the adult you. To see where things might go. Let's sit on a swing in the fairy garden. Visit museums. Do all that stuff people do when they're discovering each other. As for my raging libido, sure, there's nothing I'd like more than to back you up against that wall, peel down those sexy-as-hell jeans and sink back into you. Damn, just saying the words has me raring to go."

The front of his boxers tented and her body responded. "Let me in, Sierra. In your body. In your mind. In your heart. I want it all. I know you're scared, but I don't plan on hurting you. I've never wanted to hurt you."

Her hand flew forward on its own accord, reaching for his waistband. She had no answer for him except the stroking of her hand. Within seconds his mouth was on hers, her jeans pushed down and he filled her completely. Sierra detonated immediately. "That's it," Jack told her. "It's only like this with you. I want you to feel. To be mine. Just like I want to be yours. Let me into your life."

"My life is messy."

"I don't care." A sheen of sweat formed on his forehead. He increased the pace of his thrusts. "This is worth fighting for, wouldn't you say?"

Did he mean the sex? Or them? Or both? Thoughts became irrelevant as he soared her to new heights. Spent, both of them slid down the wall into an entangled pile on the floor. "Damn."

"Exactly." Jack grinned. He held her in his arms. "Stay longer. I'll rustle up some food and then I'll take you to get your car. I'm sure it's safe at Ingersoll's."

Her stomach grumbled at the thought of food. "Okay, but when I get my car, I'm going home. I'm not letting you convince me otherwise."

They rose, and he kissed the tip of her nose. "Let me dispose of this and get some clothes on. I'll meet you in the kitchen."

Sierra straightened her clothes, stopped at the bathroom again and made her way into the kitchen. She pressed a tall glass against the refrigerator dispenser, filling it with cold water. She drank deeply and refilled it when the contents reached halfway. She sipped again, surprised by how dehydrated she'd become. She heard the front door open and wondered if Jack had gone outside. Then she heard footsteps in the hall, a whirring noise and feet pounding down the stairs. The whirring noise got louder as it came closer.

"Jack?" she called. He couldn't be in two places at once. Her eyes darted around the room. With her military training, anything could become a weapon if she needed it.

"What are you doing here?" she heard Jack say.

"Is that any way to greet me?" A man's voice. "I've come to finish what you can't seem to manage. But first I want a drink. It was a long, bumpy flight and they had to cancel beverage service midway through."

The kitchen had two doors. Jack came in from the hall at the same time as an older version of himself stepped through from the dining room. The man's eyebrows lifted in surprise. "Now I know why nothing's finalized. You're too busy fooling around."

Jack moved to shield Sierra, but his reaction was too little, too late. His expression was pained.

"Hello, Mr. Clayton. Jack and I were just catching up." Sierra kept her voice chipper.

Mr. Clayton scowled. "That's what you call it these days?"

She held her head high and stepped out from behind Jack. Sex was sex. Nothing to be ashamed of—at least not until she reached the privacy of her own home. Then she could berate herself for falling into bed with Jack, and for wanting him as much as she had. For letting herself lose control.

Time to make one thing clear. "If you've come to buy my family's winery, you're wasting your time. I'm afraid the answer is still no."

Then she grabbed her purse, snagged Jack's keys from the counter and walked out the door.

Chapter Seventeen

After watching his Mercedes peel off and leave a trail of dust, Jack shut the kitchen door. "Thanks, Dad. A heads-up might have been nice."

His dad arched an eyebrow. "And miss the show? No wonder why you haven't closed the deal. You're too busy closing other things instead."

Jack's hands clenched, but one did not hit one's father. Even if the man deserved it. "That's crass."

"I call things the way I see them. I sent you to do a job, not fool around. Literally or figuratively. And certainly not with her." His father's arms folded into what Jack referred to as "the stance." He'd been on the receiving end of that formidable pose for as long as he could remember.

Jack opened the refrigerator door and grabbed a

bottle of water. Parched from the most wonderful afternoon and bitter at his father's intrusion, he took a swig before speaking. "They don't want to sell."

"Not acceptable." One of his dad's fingers began to tap the inside his elbow. "Now, if you tell me you're sleeping with the girl to get in good with her family, I might understand. Taylor's parents tell me you sent her back."

"As if I would ever sleep with a woman to make a deal," Jake shot back. "Don't you dare disrespect me or Sierra like that. And stuff the idea of me and Taylor. I'm not marrying her, much less dating her. I gave her a severance and sent her on her way."

"Don't tell me you're marrying—" Disgusted by the turn of events, his dad didn't finish but instead jerked his head toward the door where Sierra had exited.

Jack couldn't let the insult stand. While he hadn't allowed the idea of where he and Sierra might end up cross his mind, now that his dad had planted the idea of a future with her, Jack let it take root. He liked Sierra. The sex had been unlike anything else. When he was with her, the whole damn world fell away. He felt whole, complete, at peace. She made him laugh. "What if I do?" Jack shot back. "What if she's the perfect woman for me?"

His dad's scoff erupted into a derisive snarl. "Hardly. She's a washed-out navy pilot who couldn't cut it. Do you know where you stand with the girl?"

his father pressed. "How serious is it? Or is this some high school fantasy stuff you'll burn through? You better be sure before you embarrass yourself like before. I remember the homecoming debacle. She turned you down and embarrassed you in front of everyone." He huffed out extreme disappointment. "You have a huge future ahead of you, son. We haven't built all this—" he loosened his arms to gesture "—for nothing."

The hair on Jack's nape rose. "You built it for you and Mom. Not me."

"The company is something your mother and I built for you. It's a legacy we've created for you and your brothers."

Who'd all gone into other professions, unlike their older brother. No, when your name was Jonathan Caldwell Clayton III, better known as Jack, one followed in his father's footsteps. Jack's adherence had allowed his siblings to escape the pressure, not that they weren't overachievers themselves. One was a successful surgeon. One directed Hollywood movies and had won an Oscar.

Jack's father punched out a text. "I've let your mother know I've arrived. Is there food in this place?"

"Not that you'll want. We can go out." Jack resigned himself to the inevitable. Most likely Sierra had dropped his car at Ingersoll's and retrieved hers.

"Can you drop me off at Ingersoll's first? My car is there."

His father snorted. "You let her strand you? Haven't you learned anything?"

"I'll call an Uber. Save me the guilt trip."

His father rolled his eyes. "I'll take you once I've freshened up. Make a reservation for Miller's for a half hour from now. Tell them it's for me and they'll make room. We can discuss this matter over bourbon because we are going to solve this. We have work to do before your mother arrives Thursday for the Halloween festival. You know that's one of her favorite events."

Without waiting for an answer, his father grabbed his carry-on bag and marched from the room. The water bottle in his left hand empty, Jack tightened his fist. The clear plastic protested the pressure with hisses of air and loud scrunching. Jack tossed the crumpled remains into the recycle bin, taking no joy in landing the shot. The bottle rattled as it settled. He strode upstairs, softening his step as he reached the second-floor hallway. He shut the bedroom door behind him, the lock latching with a quiet click. Slamming the door would serve no purpose besides revealing his anger, and the last thing Jack wanted was to give his father any more ammunition.

He straightened bedsheets that held Sierra's scent before he jumped into the en suite shower. He let the spiced soap and hot water rinse her from his skin.

Where did he stand with her? She'd had a panic attack and they'd landed in bed. They weren't dating. They weren't anything, really. Not even friends by the traditional definition of the word. Damn it. He hated when his father made sense.

Clayton Holdings was Jack's inheritance. He had a cushy office back in Portland waiting for him, and the clock ticked down until his return. Sierra's job and family was here. She wouldn't follow him to the West Coast. He wasn't planning on staying in Beaumont.

Maybe she and Jack were, what was the word? *Star-crossed.* Maybe they'd been ill-fated lovers from the beginning, never meant to be. Then and now their lives were far too different. Their goals and aspirations had little in common. But that didn't matter to his heart.

Jack closed his eyes. He pictured her smile. Her brown eyes. The way her skin had glistened when slick with sweat. He brushed his teeth with a mint-flavored paste, vanquishing the sweetness he'd tasted and enjoyed from between her thighs. He'd never expected to find her when he'd started buying properties in Beaumont. Now it seemed he once again had to let her go.

After directing a sad smile to the forlorn guy reflected in the mirror, Jack girded his loins and went downstairs to locate his dad. He had business to take care of.

Chapter Eighteen

The SUV's version of Siri read aloud Sierra's mom's text. The Australian voice told Sierra that her sister, Zoe, and niece Megan were headed to the farmhouse for dinner, and that her mom hoped Sierra would join them. "Sure," Sierra dictated back. "I'm on my way home now."

For it being the Monday evening following the her running out of Jack's, it had been amazingly a good day. Her therapist had provided some breathing exercises for Sierra to try, and coupled with the cognitive behavior therapy she'd been doing since her first appointment, Sierra had managed to go to Boeing to fill out her employment paperwork and meet some of the other members of the team, even though she wouldn't join them until January. Sierra liked her team, who had pilot nicknames such as

Batman, Left Eye, Meteor and Old Joe. She was the youngest member and one of two women, and they'd all eaten lunch together. Sierra told them she'd prefer to go by Sierra rather than "Tahoe," her call sign. "It's based on my SUV and because it's a mountain in the Sierra Nevada chain," she'd explained. "Not that exciting."

She'd listened to the jumbo jets taking off from Lambert International Airport and not had a panic attack. She'd managed to sit in the flight simulator. The project she'd agreed to work on was exciting and she actually looked forward to it. The company had multiple government contracts to make flying safer and more accurate for servicemen and women and to ensure America had a strong fighting force. Sierra may have left the navy, but she cared about America's national security.

She wished that she could share the project with her family, beyond the fact that she'd had a great day. Zoe was already at the house when Sierra arrived home after a traffic-filled hour drive. Yeah, she'd have to find an apartment in St. Louis County.

Her mom had pulled out all the stops for dinner: a succulent pork roast, baked potatoes, steamed green beans, salad and rolls from the bakery on Main. "You still had time to do this and work?" Sierra asked.

"Oh, Zoe's employees held the fort down today.

Your father and I had errands to run," her mom said. "Take those in."

Sierra carried the green beans into the dining room. Their dad already sat at the head of the table. "Hey, Dad."

"Hello." When he smiled, Sierra recognized he was having one of his down days. Her phone buzzed, and Sierra reached into her jeans pocket and retrieved the device so she could turn it off. She had seventeen texts from Jack all saying a version of "call me please; it's urgent" and five missed calls, all purposefully ignored. He'd been send them since Saturday night, but these were all from today. On her way back to the kitchen, she turned the phone off and left the device on the counter.

Over dinner, Megan talked about her Daisy troop meeting. Sierra half listened, sensing something was going on. Her mom acted too chipper, as if she were intent on keeping the conversation upbeat. Following dessert, her mom waited until Zoe had settled Megan upstairs to watch a Disney movie before speaking what was on her mind.

"I don't know any other way to say this but to rip off the bandage and do it. I've decided to sell the winery."

"What?" Sierra heard herself gasp, but the words she spoke seemed to fall in a vacuum, coming out as if she were speaking like Charlie Brown's teacher. Worse, she experienced a sense of suspended animation, like before the accident, when she'd realized the plane would crash, and no matter how skilled she was, there was nothing she could do to stop it. The plane was going to fall out of the sky; the best she could do was try to control how and where it landed. "You can't sell."

"It's negotiated and the contract signed as of this afternoon. Both Jackie and the lawyer said it's an amazing deal and we'd be fools not to take it. So we did."

Jackie was Sierra's sister-in-law who was the top producer for her real estate agency.

"Mom," Sierra protested. Sierra wished Zoe would say something, but her sister appeared stunned into silence.

Her mom fidgeted with the edge of the place mat. "I spoke with both your brothers this morning. Your dad and I don't need any of your blessing, but as you two are the most impacted, I asked them to let me tell you myself. They're in agreement. It's time to sell."

"You can't. What about the house? It's part of the winery holdings." Sierra waved at the room. How many meals had these walls seen? "This is your home. Dad's home."

"We're allowed to stay here and live for as long as we'd like. The money we'll earn from selling will pay off our debts and allow me to continue your father's treatment. The cookie store is paid for, as are the cars in the garage. So Zoe, the store is yours and safe. But we've mortgaged the winery and the house to the hilt. After I sell, I'll be debt free with money in the bank."

"Why didn't you tell me about your financial straits earlier?" Angry, Sierra fought the urge to stand up and pace. "I could have done something. I have savings."

"As Mr. Clayton pointed out yesterday when he came to the house, we are beyond that point. We have creditors circling and we've been able to hold them off so far. I have to correct your father's and my financial ship and set it to rights. They had these spreadsheets and... Frankly, when Mr. Clayton showed me, it was humiliating to learn how bad I let things get."

Yesterday Sierra had worked all day. Damn Jack. He and his father had taken advantage of their parents when she'd been too busy to know what was going on.

Zoe caught her gaze. Her sister appeared blindsided. "I'm going to kill Jack and his father," Sierra announced. "He had no right to investigate us. To use your finances against you. To coerce you into selling. Surely we had options."

"I dealt mainly with his father, although they were both quite pleasant about the whole thing," her mom said. "It's Jack who insisted we can stay here as long as we wanted. The rent is one hundred dollars a year. That's extremely generous."

"Why wouldn't Jack be nice when he's getting exactly what he wanted? I saw the map in his office. Jamestown is a huge hole in the middle of his ambitious holdings. He wants our vines."

"Vines your father can't tend. We're going to have to hire someone to do the pruning. We're getting millions. And we can live here as long as we want."

"And then what?" Sierra demanded. "They take over our home? Your fairy garden?" She would not think of what she and Jack had done there. "Will they turn this place into a B&B if they don't bulldoze it down? And what about Dad's cars? Are they taking those too?"

"No. Those belong to you kids. We've always said that, and we'll have to decide what to do with the collection, whether we keep it or sell it. You know the Museum of Transportation would love to add your dad's cars to its collection. We've had a standing offer from the museum board for years, underwritten by one of their major donors. It's nothing we have to worry about right this moment. But yes, at some point the house won't belong to us after your dad and I move out. At some point, we won't be able to stay here. He'll need a memory unit, and the best ones are in St. Louis County. I'll want to visit him. I can live with Nelson. They have that in-law suite and your brother said I'm always welcome."

Sierra blinked. This was moving too far, too fast. Her mom had discussed moving in with their older brother?

"Mom." Zoe spoke then. She appeared on the verge of tears. "If you go, I'll be here by myself."

"Not for a long time. Your dad and I aren't going anywhere anytime soon." Their mom tried to reassure Zoe, but it didn't work.

Zoe's lip trembled. "Why am I in Beaumont if my family isn't here? Ted was right. I've always wanted to run the shop, but it's held me here at the expense of doing something, anything else. Now you and Dad are leaving. Nelson's in Kirkwood. Vance is in Chicago. Sierra needs to be in St. Louis, so she might as well move into Kirkwood too. That leaves me here, out in Beaumont by myself. Alone."

"The shop is yours," her mother said. "You could always sell it. Or close it and open it elsewhere. Kirkwood has a lovely downtown that would support a cookie store."

Zoe wrung her hands. "I can't deal with this." She stood and carried her dessert plate into the kitchen. After a clatter when the plate went into the sink, Sierra heard footsteps climbing the stairs.

Her mom appeared every one of her sixty-something years. Sierra understood. Deep down she truly did. But that didn't mean the delivery hadn't sucked. "You could have discussed this with us first," she told her mother. "I know it's your decision, but

MICHELE DUNAWAY 245

finding out Jamestown isn't ours anymore is like a rocket coming out of the blue. I'm supposed to work there this upcoming weekend."

"It's ours until the offer settles. That does take a few weeks to run through the title company."

"It's theirs in all but the closing and money changing hands," Sierra said. "I'm not going back there. I'm done. I have no desire to see him."

"Our selling shouldn't change how Jack feels about you or you him," her mom said. "He asked about you. It's clear he cares."

"He cares about buying the last puzzle piece and going back to Portland as fast as his plane can carry him." Sierra shook vigorously, as if by moving her head from side to side she could somehow turn back time. "He's lucky I don't throttle him. I'm trained in hand-to-hand combat. He knows what not selling meant to me. He took advantage of you."

"Sierra." Her mom's tone insinuated Sierra was being ridiculous. "Let me show you the terms and you'll see we squeezed them good. We got way more than they expected to give. It helps that we have good attorneys and an ace agent for a daughter-in-law. It's a fantastic offer. And if you want, since Zoe is getting the store, the Shelby Cobra is yours."

"I gave him a fair offer for the Cobra," her dad blurted out as a word caught his attention. He smiled at everyone happily. "Would you like to see it? It's a 1967 427 S/C. The man sold it to me instead of me charging him to repair it. I'll take you for a ride later."

"Not tonight, dear," her mother said. She covered her mouth with her hands, lest her husband see how her lips quivered. Sierra rested her forehead on her fingers, her head pounding. Her mom was right. Sierra's dad would need more and more help.

When the disease had first manifested, he'd been in the doctor's office for a wellness visit, and he'd been unable to fill in the blanks on the health forms. Then he'd stared at the cup holder, the one holding all the pens, and realized he couldn't spell the word. A PET scan and a lumbar puncture later, and the presence of Alzheimer's disease had been confirmed.

Silence reigned at the table, each to their own thoughts. What more could be said? The winery was sold. Zoe arrived with Megan in tow, took in the scene and burst into tears.

"What's wrong, Mommy?" Megan asked.

"I'm sad, that's all. Mommy got some bad news. It's fine. Nothing to worry about. It's a school night and you need a bath. If you're giving hugs, hand them out so we can go."

Understanding that her grandfather didn't know who she was today, Megan hugged only her grandmother and Sierra. Less than a minute later, Sierra heard the back door slam closed. The reverberations seemed louder than normal. "Well," she told her mom. "I have places I have to be too."

Her mother must have read something in Sierra's expression, because her expression turned pleading. "Sierra," her mom warned. "It's done. It's going to be good for us."

"How?" Sierra replied. "You always taught me decisions should never be about money. I know you did this for Dad. You need the money and really didn't have a choice. But in the end, we let them win. We surrendered. He used me. He beat us. I want him to rue the day he messed with me."

"Sierra. Don't do anything stupid. If you look at this logically—"

Sierra stood. "I'm fine, Mom. You don't need to worry about me." Sierra grabbed her dessert plate and headed into the kitchen. No, Jack was the one who should be worried. He wouldn't even know what hit him. She'd crashed and burned once. The second time shouldn't be scary now that she'd had the practice. This wasn't like a kamikaze suicide mission. She'd survive whatever came next, one way or the other.

But one thing was clear—it was time to take care of Jerk Clayton once and for all.

Chapter Nineteen

Jack hated dinner parties, especially the kind where he had to wear dress slacks, a button-down and a sport coat. He liked jeans. Henley shirts. Even the long-sleeve flannels so ubiquitous to Beaumont, which would be perfect for a clear fall night like this.

But once his father had secured the written commitment for Jamestown yesterday and the signed paperwork today, he'd decided a dinner party was in order. His dad had invited some of his old cronies, some of his business contemporaries and the members of the chamber of commerce and the city council. This party was proof that, with enough money, one could work miracles, like buying a beloved family winery. Or finding a vendor who could pitch a party canopy and cater a buffet dinner for forty out on the B&B lawn. The exclusive invites had gone out at noon and by 1:00 p.m. everyone had responded yes. The guests sat around five tables covered with twinkling votives and fronds of greenery, enjoying steak and chicken, the typical accompaniments and a full open bar.

Everyone knew, when Jonathan Caldwell Clayton II beckoned, the wisest thing to do was drop plans and rearrange schedules, especially when Jack's father spared no expense. Even his mother had arrived two days early, bringing with her an unwelcome surprise.

"Isn't this lovely?" Taylor said. She sat next to Jack, wearing a long-sleeved bright floral maxi dress with a deep V neckline, both front and back. Multiple thin gold strands draped over into the valley between her breasts, but Taylor didn't raise Jack's temperature or capture his interest any more than the propane heaters working overtime.

Jack gritted his teeth. He'd asked his office manager to find him a new administrative assistant, and Doris had emailed the résumés of her top three candidates. In a funk since Saturday, Jack had ignored the files. He hadn't done much since Sierra walked out, minus retrieve his car, listen to his father's lecture and watch as the man played his trump card and captured a winery. The whole thing left a bad taste in Jack's mouth, as did the thousands of unanswered messages he'd left and the texts he kept sending

Sierra. He deserved Sierra's wrath. When it came down to it, like in high school, he'd been weak. He'd caved. Done what his father expected. He'd never forgive his dad for hurting her. He couldn't regret making love to her. That memory would have to carry him, would always be a reminder of how once again he'd messed up.

Taylor placed her hand on Jack's arm. "Your dad's about to make a speech."

He wanted to answer "Whoopee, who gives a shit," but instead Jack lifted the glass containing bourbon neat, exactly two fingers worth. The fire of handcrafted whiskey burned down his throat as his dad spoke about something or other—Jack tuned out. His dad could be long-winded and verbose on most occasions, but tonight he kept his speech short, for once not gloating as he thanked everyone for being present and received their toasts for the Beaumont project's success.

Taylor rubbed her fingers lightly on his sleeve. "You'll be able to go home now. Things can go back to normal. I'll get us symphony tickets. You'd like that."

While he loved listening to Yo-Yo Ma, Jack wasn't a diehard classical music fan. "You have no idea what it is I like." He moved his arm forward, lifting the bourbon glass and shaking Taylor's hand from his arm. She rested her palm on the white linen tablecloth, the long red nails contrasting like blood on paper. She glanced up. "Hello, Mrs. Clayton."

"Hello, Taylor dear." Jack's mom smiled her greeting before pinning her gaze on her son. "Jack, may I speak with you please?"

Feeling like a petulant three-year-old, Jack followed his mother toward a quiet corner near the edge of the tent. He leashed his frustration. "Yes? Was there something you needed?"

His mother studied him. "Does a mother need anything to want to speak with her oldest son? Especially when she hasn't seen her son for any length of quality time in the last few months?"

"No." He checked his hand before he dragged his fingers through his hair and made it spike uncontrollably. He took a sip of small craft bourbon instead.

"You don't seem happy," she observed.

No kidding, Jack thought. He was miserable. He debated what to tell his mom. She'd been content to be in the dark in regards to business and instead ran the social and family aspects of her marriage. But Jack couldn't stay silent. Not this time. Not when it had cost him the woman he'd fallen for before the relationship truly began. "At what price do we do things?" he asked as he struggled for the appropriate words. "When does the deal we make become too much and have too high a cost?"

She blinked. "I'm not certain I understand.

Wasn't all this what you wanted? You'd mapped everything out ever since the idea's inception. You took it and ran."

"Not all of it, and not this." He let more liquid fire burn down the back of his throat. "Certainly not dating or marrying Taylor. Drop that from your mind. I sent her back for a reason. I don't know why she's here, but it's not going to work. She's not the one for me."

His mother didn't appear too upset. "That's an easy fix. But I sense your issue is deeper than that. Something changed you while you were here. Or someone."

His mother had always stayed on the business sidelines, but that didn't mean she hadn't been an intuitive, hands-on mom to him and his brothers. She sensed there was more, as she had the day Jack returned home following Sierra's rejection of his homecoming invite. Thank goodness he hadn't done one of those full-on homecoming proposals like kids did now and had only handed her a rose. He would have been even more humiliated after she said no had some video gone viral.

Sierra, the one woman he'd always wanted and the one woman whose heart he couldn't have. She'd stolen his long ago, and he'd hoped and prayed after they'd made love they could continue to explore the feelings they had for each other.

But maybe his feelings had been one-sided all along. Jack shook his head. "I'm fine."

"Darling," his mom said, but at that moment came a loud clatter of dishes, and then a gasp from the crowd, followed by the murmur of voices that drowned out the string quartet his father had managed to secure last minute.

"Jack Clayton," a voice he knew intimately shouted. "Show your face, you coward."

Sierra charged toward him, the waiter clearing plates retrieving several he'd dropped. She stopped about thirty feet away, blocked by two of Jack's father's security guards. She wore jeans, a long-sleeved T-shirt and tennis shoes.

Jack walked toward her, into the fray. "Let her pass," Jack called.

Did he imagine it, or did a curious hush fall over the crowd? She strode forward, stopping within an arm's length. They stood in sight of everyone, and he could easily reach out and draw her into an embrace. Not that he did. "Of course she'd make a scene," he heard Taylor mutter.

"She has a name," he snarled in response. "Sierra."

"Jack. Enjoying your celebratory party?" Anger emanated from Sierra's every pore. She was magnificent.

Jack noted his dad had moved closer. "It's my father's party."

"Of course, hide behind dear old dad. Pathetic."

"Sierra, can we talk in private?" He had so much he wanted to say. He reached for her elbow but she sidestepped him.

"I won't be here long." Two fingers pulled a wad of bills from her back pocket. "You forgot this when you fleeced my parents."

The circle of curious onlookers grew bigger as Sierra reached forward and slapped what appeared to be a thick stack of twenties into his hand, as if she'd raided an ATM. Automatically his fist closed around the bills so they didn't fall and scatter.

The moment her hands were free, Sierra reached for an open wine bottle, a half-full bottle of Jamestown Norton. She tipped the bottle back and took a sip. Then she wiped her mouth with the back of her hand. "There. That'll give your dad some more fodder to use against me. Sierra James. So unhinged and uncouth."

"Sierra, what is this? Let's go somewhere private and…"

"No need. I'm leaving. I just wanted to make sure you got your proceeds. After all, you won the bet. You got the winery and you had me. But no more."

She tipped the bottle, and the rest of the wine poured out, splashing over Jack's hands and shoes. He jumped back, the bills capturing the red liquid as Sierra acted like a vengeful goddess casting down judgment.

"I'd say screw you, Jerk Clayton, but sadly I already did that. So go to hell, Jack, and never come near me or my family again." She saw Taylor and rolled her eyes. She shook her head with disgust and Jack watched as a complete calm came over her, as if her previous actions had been all a deliberate dramatic performance designed for maximum reaction. "You really are something, aren't you? As if I needed any additional proof of my poor judgment where you're concerned. Once an ass, always an ass. You're not worth the dust on my shoes."

With that, she spun around and walked away. When she got to Randy, she gave him one derisive glance and a "you're still nothing but shit, Randy" and passed by him before Randy could react. Randy appeared dumfounded, Paula gasped and Jack couldn't help but start to smile. Damn, but she was magnificent, forcing the onlookers to part before her. She swept through them with her chin high, doing what Jack had always been afraid to do. She'd taken a stand and gone out swinging. Jack had always done what his parents and friends wanted. He wished he'd had half her courage in high school, half her courage now. She dealt with things head on, including the things holding her back. Sadly, he was one of them. Her words had shredded him. "Go to hell. Never come near me again." He'd gained a winery but lost what he really wanted. Her.

She handed the bottle to an astounded waiter.

"Don't forget to recycle." Then she disappeared from sight.

"Well." His father gestured to the quartet, which began playing something up-tempo. "Everyone have another drink. Show's over." The crowd moved away. Even Taylor moved to the other side of the tent.

"Who was that?" his mother asked Jack once he returned to where she'd remained standing.

"That's Sierra James. She won't have me." Jack threw the damp bills onto the table, creating spreading spots of purplish color. She'd handed him close to $500. Was that what the pot had been for the winner? Was this the price for her virginity? Sixteen years ago, the amount received would have been a small fortune. No wonder the guys had bought in. Jack's stomach mimicked that of a seasick sailor.

His father approached. "You sure know how to pick them. What the hell, Jack? Could you not handle her?"

"Sierra was blindsided by the purchase of her family winery. She's deservedly angry."

"The place belongs to her parents, not her. She's always been a high-strung mess. Couldn't even make it in the navy."

Jack's final thread of patience snapped like a bow strung too tight. "She has PTSD from her accident, a crash in which her actions saved her life and that of her student. When did you become a snob, Dad? When did you change? Or is it that I'm finally old enough to look at you differently? See that you aren't the hero I once thought?"

His mother gasped. "Jack!"

His dad sputtered. "Don't make this my fault. It's her crazy rubbing off."

A serenity descended, as if the heavens had opened and beamed through a single, bright light. "You don't need me. But I need her. She makes me better. She opens my eyes. When I'm with her, the world drops away. But this sale has ruined any chance I had with her. I can't do this anymore."

"Jack, don't do something you'll regret," his mom's gentle voice warned. "Think things through."

But for once Jack wanted to throw himself into the mercy of the abyss. He'd already hit rock bottom. How much worse could falling further be? "I'm thinking straight for the first time ever." Sierra's bravery, even if sourced from pure fury, inspired. "I no longer want to work on this project. It's all yours, Dad. I quit."

Chapter Twenty

"We're quite a pair."

"What do you mean?" Sierra asked. They stood in the cookie store, where her younger sister loaded chocolate chip cookies into the display case bright and early before the store opened Friday morning. It had been a week since the winery sale and Sierra's confrontation with Jack.

"Our love lives being the talk of the town," Zoe said. "I told Jared I didn't think it was wise if we dated."

"You didn't. Zoe, why?" As soon as Zoe set the tray down, Sierra wrapped her in a hug. "It's clear he liked you."

"There's too much drama surrounding the fact he's my daughter's principal. The grief the other moms keep giving me. It's too intense. Too soon. We just met a month or so ago."

Sierra's heart broke for her sister. "You've been divorced for a while."

"It doesn't matter. Did I tell you how brave I think you are? You dumped Jack even though deep down you like him. You're an inspiration."

"I don't know if I like Jerk Clayton," Sierra protested. "And you shouldn't follow my example. It was rather ill-planned, even if sort of well executed. His face..."

His face had been full of hurt. Sierra tried to brush aside any guilt. They were through. She'd heard he'd returned to Portland.

Zoe paused skeptically. "You have a terrible poker face. You can't even say his name without sounding wistful."

"Okay, fine. I can't get him out of my mind. But it's done. You, on the other hand, should not listen to those catty moms. Go to the festival with Jared. You shouldn't have said no or told him that you didn't want to see him. Undo it."

"I can't. Those moms are right. It's too complicated." Zoe followed Sierra back into the kitchen and, as a timer chimed, she removed sprinkle cookies from the oven. "As kids, we hope we'll get everything we want. As adults, we're more realistic."

Sierra turned sharply toward her sister. "Are you saying you don't want the store?"

"I don't know what I want anymore," Zoe admitted. "This whole thing with our mom and dad selling the winery has me reevaluating everything. Why do I live here? I'm geographically challenged in finding a man, not that I necessarily want one. I liked how Jared made me laugh. But we clicked too easily. There has to be a catch somewhere down the line."

"What if there's not?" Sierra asked. "What if what you and Jared have is real?"

"I don't know. He asked the same when we talked and I told him things were moving far too fast. He said he didn't like the gossip either. But he agreed to back off. We'll attend the Halloween festival separately. Right now I'm more worried about you. What if Jack's your special someone?"

Sierra gave an unladylike snort. "Andrea texted and said she ran into him during a meeting her company had with Clayton Holdings. He's wrapping up some project in the Willamette Valley."

"And then?"

Sierra shrugged. "I don't know or care. Andrea said he quit. But at the same time she can't confirm if he's really no longer with the family company."

"Would that change your mind about him?"

Sierra shook her head. She was still unpacking her actions with her therapist. "No. My heart wants to fall head over heels for him. But I'm too practical. I know it can't work. Right now I'm making progress with my therapy and that comes first. Standing my ground that night, even throwing down the money, was cathartic. It felt like a huge break-through. At that moment, I was never more sane. It was like one of those 'I'm back' realizations. I can conquer everything because all the power is within me. I just have to tap it."

"I wish I had your strength," Zoe said. She ges-tured. "I'm wondering if I should sell this place. Move into the city. Start over in a place where ev-eryone doesn't know me. Mom's right. This shop would work in a downtown like Kirkwood where there's heavy foot traffic."

"We all want you to be happy. Scout out some places. No reason to rush. You've expanded into shipping to the continental forty-eight. And you saw that Jack's company wants to put your cook-ies into the hotel. Don't pass on that opportunity because of me."

Zoe took a deep breath. "I'm not as brave as you. Since our online business is booming, I might pass. I don't want to overextend."

"You don't have to decide now," Sierra told her. "The deal allows Mom and Dad to keep their house and their land for as long as they want. Jack's dad came by the house yesterday to discuss something. I stayed upstairs lest I tell him off."

"That family's had comeuppance coming for a while," Zoe told her. "I'm glad it's you who gave it to them."

Sierra glanced at the clock. It was almost ten,

which meant they'd open to customers soon. "Look, about you and Jared? Ask him to the dance Saturday night. How else are you going to figure out if this week made you forget him, or if it made you want him more?"

"I might," Zoe conceded. "I'm glad you're here, you know? I'd hug you but then we'd have to wash up."

Sierra grinned. "What brought that out? But yeah, me too. And no matter what, I'll always be a text away." And she'd get through this. Jack and she might be history, same for their family winery, but Sierra had her friends and her family. A good job starting after the holidays. She'd do more than survive. She planned to thrive.

Hello freedom. Jack glanced around his executive office, now stripped of personal effects. He'd meant every word of what he'd told his dad. He'd quit Clayton Holdings with a "I'm gone as soon as I shift my projects," and he didn't plan on looking back. Of course, at first, his dad hadn't believed him.

After the party his dad had tried all his favorite tactics, but for once Jack had held firm. The next morning he'd left the Mercedes at the B&B for his mother's use, taken an Uber to the St. Louis airport and caught the first commercial flight to Portland. Minus communicating through work emails to shift his other projects around, Jack hadn't talked to his father since that night, and certainly not about the Beaumont project.

Which was why he found himself shocked and surprised when he glanced up and saw his father standing in the doorway. His dad surveyed the bare spaces on the walls where diplomas and certificates had once hung, lone nails poking out marking their absence. "So you're really doing this. Leaving the company."

"I am," Jack said. He wasn't certain what he would do next, but luckily, given his strong financial position, he had options. For once he'd stand on his own, and he was excited to sort through the ideas he had percolating.

His father put his hand on a file cabinet and swiped, as if checking for dust. "Is there anything I can do to change your mind?"

"Step down?" Jack quipped.

His dad seemed older than he had been a week ago. "Is that what it would take?"

"Dad, you're not seriously considering it, so drop it." Jack fought his mounting frustration. "I want different things now. This company is your dream, not mine."

"It was once. This is because of the girl. You'd throw all this away for one girl?"

"Her name is Sierra. Sierra James. And yes, I would. But I'm not doing it for her. I'm doing it for me. I'm smart. I can build my own business from the ground up. If you can do it, so can I. I'm ready to prove it, not to you, but to myself. It's time to fly the nest, so to speak."

"I wish you wouldn't. You're making a mistake."

"For the first time in a while, I'm confident I'm not."

"You really think she'll forgive you?"

He meant Sierra. Jack glanced out the window at the glistening water. He'd miss this view of the Willamette River, but it wasn't enough to stay for. "Maybe not, but I have to try. And to do that, I'm going to have to be there and not working for you."

"Okay, then," his dad said. "I support you."

"I don't need your support," Jack told him. Although it was nice to hear.

"No, you don't." Jack's father suddenly appeared even older than five minutes ago. "You're your own man, son. You've done great for this company and I hoped you'd take over. I don't like that you're leaving. I hope you come back someday. But I want you happy. Your mother and I both do. I have to be a father first for once."

Jack refused to let his resolve soften, but the words touched him. "Thanks. I appreciate that. Was there anything else?"

His dad shook his head. "No. Thanks for all your help in delegating your workload. It's appreciated."

"I do love you," Jack told his father. "You're a

good dad. But I want more. Fair warning, when I do win her back, you'll be nice. You'll behave and welcome her with open arms."

His mom came into doorway. "Trust me, I'll make sure of it. Jon, are you ready?" When her husband nodded, she came over and planted a kiss on Jack's cheek. "Let's get lunch tomorrow, you and me. Can you squeeze that in?"

"Of course." Jack watched his parents leave. He hadn't asked who was running the Beaumont project. One thing he'd learned early in life was that no single employee was irreplaceable. A person's work might be hard to duplicate, but empty spots got filled with new people. The world moved on. Jobs were finished and tasks completed.

However, finding the right person was often difficult and a result of trial and error. Finding the perfect one could be that proverbial needle in a haystack, or like trying to grab a half-inch, closed safety pin from a baggie of rice—one of the upcoming games kids would play at the Halloween festival.

Deep in Jack's heart he felt Sierra was his person. She was his soul mate. While they'd reconnected for what, in the grand scheme of things, people might consider a short period of time, when Jack was certain of something, he was all in.

He'd regret the loss forever if he couldn't be with her.

He prayed it wasn't too late to win her back.

Chapter Twenty-One

Around 3:00 p.m. the Halloween festival swung into high gear. A sunny, high-sixties, perfect-weather Saturday greeted those wearing costumes and playing games inside and outside Ingersoll's bright red barn.

"What shall we do next?" Dressed in her adorable ladybug costume, Sierra's niece Megan stood between her mom and Sierra. Megan held an orange plastic bucket decorated with a smiling jack-o'-lantern face. A thick layer of consolation-prize candy covered the bottom.

"What about the duck pond? Mrs. Bien set it up over there."

"Duck ponds are for babies," Megan announced. She rattled the bucket. "I'm a first-grader. I want to do the teddy bear walk."

"Don't you have enough teddy bears at home?" Sierra asked, but when Megan tugged on her hand, Sierra went willingly. Megan drew them toward a circle consisting of twenty numbers. Sierra passed over three tokens as admission, and soon musical notes of "Monster Mash" blared from nearby speakers. Everyone walked around and around until the attendant stopped the music. He called out "Number Six." Megan frowned, disappointed. She wasn't standing on that number, but her face lit up when she realized her aunt Sierra was. After being declared the winner, Sierra walked over to the prize table, and soon Megan stuck a small blue teddy bear into her bucket. Its eyes and ears looked out over the rim.

"Now what?" Sierra asked. She peered through her Ray-Bans and tugged on the sleeve of her bomber jacket. She'd dressed as an off-duty aviator, the rest of her outfit a T-shirt and hip-hugging jeans.

Dressed as Raggedy Ann, Zoe shrugged. That was the thing about festivals. Eventually you completed all the activities. "Shall we do the corn maze again?" Zoe asked.

"I'm hungry," Megan announced, as if she hadn't been filling herself with candy for the last few hours and at lunch before that.

They walked toward the picnic tables and the food vendors. Besides the taco truck, the Miller's Grill tent sold barbecue, Auntie Jayne's had assorted cookies for sale and Clara's Café offered a variety of grab-n-go sandwiches. Sierra purchased brisket sandwiches for her and Zoe, while at the same time Zoe went to the food truck and purchased tacos for Megan.

Sierra noted brisk business at the cookie booth. Across the way, in the twenty-one-and-over beer garden, a line of customers waited at La Vita è Vino Dolce's mobile self-service wine cart. Maybe she'd try Caleb Master's new wine venture later tonight, if she came back for the adults-only dance.

The sisters regrouped at a picnic table covered with a red-and-white-checkered plastic cloth. Miller's never disappointed, Sierra thought as she bit into the delicious smoked meat. To make everything finger friendly, the sandwich came with plain potato chips. Sierra wiped the excess salt from her fingers. Then she jumped as beside her, Megan squealed. "There's Anna and Lacey. Can I go see them? *Pleeeze?*" She clasped her hands together, which made the ladybug antenna above her face bounce.

"Sure," Zoe replied. Sierra watched as Megan bounded over to the two girls, who stood with their dads. Jared Dempsey, the elementary principal, gave a nod in Zoe's direction. Zoe dipped her chin in response and then bit into her sandwich.

"You don't appear happy," Sierra noted.

Zoe swallowed. "Nothing's changed between me and Jared since you and I last talked."

"I'm sorry to hear that. You should go over there. Say hi."

"I can't use Megan as an opening."

Emboldened, Sierra stood. "I can."

"Sierra, no. Don't." Behind her, Zoe rose too, her plate of food half-eaten.

But Sierra chose not to listen. Zoe needed a nudge and she'd give her one. By the time she'd reached Jared, Luke had left to purchase food. "You must be Jared. Hi, I'm Sierra, Zoe's sister and Megan's aunt."

They exchanged greetings while Zoe approached. Sierra noted how her sister's gaze drank him in. Jared had a kind face, and his expression softened as he gazed at her. "Zoe."

Sierra made an instantaneous decision, one even more urgent as she saw Randy and Paula and their brood headed toward the food court. "Come on, girls, let's go sit down."

"Hi, Zoe. I like your costume. How are you?" Jared said as Sierra ushered the girls away.

When Jared and Zoe sat down a few minutes later, Zoe appeared much happier. Luke joined them, as did his wife, Shelby, and soon they had quite the rollicking party at their picnic table.

"Sierra, you love to fly. Want to go with me in the balloon when I take the two winners up?" Shelby asked. "I could use the company."

Sierra's heart began to race. Did a trickle of sweat form? "Luke's not going?"

"I'm on dad duty," he said. "But I'm helping set up."

"I don't know," Sierra admitted. "Flying's been rough for me since the accident." Even saying the words aloud felt like progress. "I'd like to say maybe, but..."

"I saw you rush off last weekend," Shelby said. "I thought I recognized the signs. We took flying lessons together, and that wasn't like you."

"Come on, girls. Help me get the table clean so that we can go do the corn maze again." Upon Luke's words, everyone but Shelby and Sierra left the table.

"The heat and noise. It became too much. I'm in therapy and have taken baby steps," Sierra admitted. She'd known Shelby forever.

"Come help me lay out the lines," Shelby said. "We'll go from there. One thing at a time. Maybe it'll help. Be like riding a bike."

"Okay," Sierra agreed. She could do baby steps. She followed Shelby out to the field where Playgroup waited. "So you could tell?"

"Only because one of my coworkers has severe PTSD. He'd been a war correspondent before coming to work for the magazine. He photographed Syria and Ukraine, and loud noises are a trigger. We heard an avalanche last winter when out in the mountains. Mind you, we were safe, but the sound echoed. He couldn't continue the shoot. He had trouble concentrating for days."

"The symptoms are usually grouped into different types. Mine are physical and emotional reactions," Sierra said.

Shelby gestured to the lines, and Sierra placed them in the grass and straightened them. She spread out Playgroup's envelope and helped as Shelby clipped the lines to the basket. The pilot always assembled the burners, and when finished, Shelby said, "Come stand in the basket."

Nothing was firing and the balloon lay on the ground. Sierra climbed in. She fingered the thick wicker, and she ran her hand over the smooth metal frame. "I can see why you love her."

"Last fall she brought Luke and me together. Flying became a way we reconnected. You need to reconnect to yourself and to the sky."

Over by the barn, a loudspeaker announced the results of the contest and who would get a free hot-air balloon ride. People began heading their way. "How about once she gets going, you see if you can stand in the basket and take the heat?" Shelby suggested.

Why were they called baby steps? Did babies hesitate? Or was it because they had tiny legs? Sierra could stand in the basket. Experience the heat from above. Take things slow.

She stepped out and helped lay the basket on its

side. Once Luke arrived, he turned on a giant circular fan and pumped air into the envelope. Playgroup inflated, and Shelby fired the burners so that the air heated. The warmer the air, the more the envelope filled, causing Playgroup to spread out to her full glory, its sunburst pattern evident. Once the balloon stood straight as did the basket with Shelby inside, volunteers helped keep it tethered to the ground. Luke supervised, his hand on the main line. Sierra didn't run this time, and Shelby outstretched her hand. "Just stand in the basket."

Sierra's feet didn't want to move. But something inside her took over and Sierra climbed inside the wicker. Her neck angled upward, gazing into the balloon with its vibrant colors. The burners whooshed, and Sierra froze. "Breathe," Shelby shouted into her ear. "Remember when I froze during the lessons all those years ago? You told me to breathe. So breathe."

Sierra maybe caught every other word Shelby said because of the noise, but her mind filled in the rest. She put on the gloves Shelby handed her. The couple who won climbed into the basket and began chattering. Shelby turned to Sierra, reached and pulled on the lever that controlled the fuel. The burners flared. "Ready?"

A breeze hit Sierra. What went up had to come down. How many times had she replayed that nightmare? But she wanted to be fearless. She wanted to be free. She wanted to fly again. Sierra squeezed her eyes shut and gave Shelby a thumbs-up. "Ready."

With that, Shelby signaled, Luke gave orders and Playgroup lifted smoothly into the air. The world grew quiet, minus the burners and the chatter of the couple enjoying the ride. Clutching the edge, Sierra opened her eyes. Beaumont spread out before her—the town outlined to the northeast and the Missouri River beyond that. They floated over wine country, heading over Elephant Rocks and Jamestown. "How you doing?" Shelby asked.

Sierra made a poor attempt at a joke as she worked on her breathing. "Let's see how I do on the way down."

"You're doing great. You got this," Shelby said. She chatted easily with her guests.

As the balloon soared higher, Sierra's shoulders lost some of their tension. Her fingers loosened their grips. Riding in Playgroup was nothing compared with being in a fighter jet. But she was flying. They soared over fields and towns, heading southwest. Shelby piloted Playgroup as if it were an extension of her arm. The hour flew by, and as Shelby began to set the balloon down in a field, Sierra could see the chase vehicle at the ready and behind it, Zoe's car and one for the winners.

Things on the ground grew bigger and the ground rose to greet them, and as the fear came, Sierra fought it back with everything she had. She watched a hawk soar high. Below five deer raced through the field, scared by the colorful creature descending from the sky.

Then came the thud, and while the basket hopped once, it never tipped. Shelby stuck the landing, and behind her, the rest of the envelope began to fall. "I did it," Sierra screamed. "Stick it, universe!"

"Step one." Shelby gave Sierra a high five before turning to high-five the basket's other occupants.

Sierra climbed out and dropped to her knees and kissed the ground, laughing and sputtering as she spit out a few pieces of grass. She knew there would be many more steps and challenges to come before she could climb back into a cockpit. PTSD didn't simply disappear. She'd have to live with it the rest of her life. But she would overcome. She'd get stronger. Baby steps. One thing, one day at a time.

Zoe came running across the field, her costume's white apron flattening around her front. "You did it! You flew!" Her sister cried tears of joy that streamed down her face, ruining the black lines she'd painted under her eyes. Sierra stood and Zoe spun her in a huge hug.

"I did." Behind them, Luke began to unhook the basket from the envelope. "I should help them pack. Where's Megan?"

"I left her with our mom. Well, Lacey too. Jared asked me to the dance tonight."

"Are you going?"

Zoe followed Sierra over to the lines. "I haven't decided."

Following Luke's instruction, Sierra began to gather the ropes. Soon they had stowed the balloon in its custom trailer. Sierra followed Zoe to her car. High on the adrenaline from reaching this touchstone, she voiced her idea. "You go, I'll go. Will that work?" When her sister hesitated, Sierra played her ace. "I flew. I faced a fear. You gotta do the same. I'll be right there."

"Okay," Zoe agreed. "I'll do it. We'll do it."

"Good." From here forward, Sierra planned to grab life with both hands.

God help anyone who got in her way.

Chapter Twenty-Two

"Aw, will you look at that?" Zoe said. She pointed over to where their cousin Andrea stood on the dance floor with Caleb. The song had changed, but they hadn't moved. "That looks promising. I knew those two were meant to be."

Sierra gave her sister a tiny push. "Which is why you should go talk to Jared. I want to swing by Jamestown on my way home. The stars always look better from there, and the planets are in a line starting in about an hour. I want to see them one last time from the deck, you know? You stay here. Make the most of the night. Seriously. Talk to the man."

Leaving her sister, Sierra drove to Jamestown. She keyed her way through the gate, parking on the upper lot. She entered the building, turned off the alarm and locked the door behind her. Guided by the security lights, she went behind the bar and grabbed an open bottle of Norton and a clean glass. She went out onto the deck and chose a chair.

From this viewpoint, the night sky spread out like a starry blanket. She poured herself a glass and used the app on her phone to scan the night sky, noting the constellations near the sliver of moon. When she'd been a girl, she'd sat out here and dreamed of being an astronaut. Once escrow closed, this after-hours view would no longer be hers. She'd have to make tonight's memory last.

Far below a car turned onto the drive. Headlights marked its progress as it came through the gate and up through the drive. At first, she thought it might be the sheriff, come to check on the place. But she recognized that particular Mercedes convertible.

She remained seated, wondering why the hell Jack was at Jamestown long after the venue closed. She couldn't tell if he checked the front doors that she'd locked, but a few moments later she heard his footsteps along the path, and then thumps on the stair treads as he came onto the deck. She flipped her phone over, trying to hide the purple glow. "Si-erra."

Too late. He'd seen her. She tried to calm her racing heart. "Jack. What are you doing here?"

"Your sister told me where you were. I went to the dance looking for you."

Her senses drank him in. "We were never going to dance together. You got your money. I don't even know if we have things to say to each other."

"You may not, but I have things to say. First and foremost, I'm going to apologize. Then I'm going to tell you I quit my job. Finally, I'm going to tell you that I love you. I've always loved you, even when I didn't even know what true love was. But I know now it's you. I can't fix this." He waved his hand indicating the winery. "But I want most desperately to fix us. Please forgive me."

"You love me." Sierra let that sink in before frowning. "Wait. You quit your job? What are you thinking?" Overwhelmed by all of his announcements—and he loved her!—she set her wineglass down.

He drew her out of her chair, standing her on her feet. "About what part? My quitting? My dad went around my back on my project. He tornadoed his way through. I didn't stand up for you then, but I'm doing it now. As for my loving you, I told my mom you're the one I want. Not just for today but forever. I'll grovel as much as needed because I want to win you back."

A fire lit inside Sierra. She walked on air, as if she'd grown wings or turned into a hot-air balloon herself. His words created a sensation akin to the giddiness of flying. "You're crazy, you know it? Absolutely bat shit crazy."

"About you, yes. I want to start fresh. We'll face

whatever comes together. You may not feel about me the way I feel about you, but I'm hoping that if we take it slow, maybe one day you'll return my feelings and…"

She stopped him by pressing her hand onto the side of his face. "Jack."

"Yeah?"

The stubble was delicious beneath her fingertips. Her heart overfilled. "I wrote your name in my diary when I was in kindergarten that you were the one I wanted. I love you too, even though at times it goes against my better judgement."

"I promise to make that up to you. Over and over and over."

"Then kiss me, will you?"

"Your wish is my command." He brought his lips to hers in a kiss that sent her spiraling. She clung to him, every pore breathing him in and claiming him as hers.

"You love me," he said. He kissed down her neck.

"Even when you were a jerk and pulled my pigtails. Even when I was telling you to go to hell. Deep down, it's always been you."

He held her gaze. "I promise not to be a jerk to you ever again. I want to be your man, Sierra. I want to love you forever. I heard you flew today." His fingers slid off the jacket and pulled up her T-shirt. His hands slid underneath the fabric.

"I did. Are you planning on making me fly again?"

"Every day from now until forever if you'll let me. Ever made love out here on the deck?"

His hands palmed her breasts as his tongue circled her ear. "Of course not. But there's always a first time."

"I want a lifetime of firsts with you."

"Good, because I love you and want the same."

Later, as they lay entwined on top of their clothes, the night breeze cooling their heated skin, Sierra lifted her head from Jack's chest. "Jack?"

"Yeah?"

"I think you should eventually go back to work for your dad."

"Why? I told you..."

She stuck her forefinger in his mouth. He sucked on it as she began to kiss down his chest. She raised her head. "Here's the deal. If I'm marrying you, like I wrote in that diary..."

"You seriously did that, huh?" he said before kissing her finger again.

Her heart overjoyed and complete, she laughed. "I did. I can show you."

"I'm holding you to that. As for you marrying me, you always were the smartest person in the room. This proves it."

"And don't you ever forget it." She captured him in her hand, lowered her mouth and loved on him. She brought him to the brink before saying, "So, Jack?"

He could only moan. She grinned. "I didn't give you the reason why you should work for your dad. If I'm with you forever, then I want my damn winery back. I might even trade it for a certain Shelby Cobra that has my name on it."

"No need." Jack laughed and flipped her over so she lay beneath him. "You can have whatever you want, including your winery and my convertible, even if not as rare as yours. As long as you realize that we're a package deal."

"I love you."

"And I you." The lips nibbling on her earlobe promised wicked and wonderful things to come, always and forever. "Mine is yours, my love. Mine is yours."

And by loving her, he made her fly.

* * * * *

*For more reunion romances, look for these other
Harlequin Special Edition stories:*

What Happens in the Air
by Michele Dunaway

Hometown Reunion
by Christine Rimmer

Valentines for the Rancher
by Kathy Douglass

*Available now wherever
Harlequin Special Edition books are sold!*

COMING NEXT MONTH FROM

H HARLEQUIN®

SPECIAL EDITION™

#2977 SELF-MADE FORTUNE
The Fortunes of Texas: Hitting the Jackpot • by Judy Duarte
Heiress Gigi Fortune has the hots for her handsome new lawyer! Harrison Vasquez may come from humble beginnings, but they have so much fun—in and out of bed! If only she can convince him their opposite backgrounds are the perfect ingredients for a shared future...

#2978 THE MARINE'S SECOND CHANCE
The Camdens of Montana • by Victoria Pade
The worst wound Major Dalton Camden ever received was the day Marli Abbott broke his heart. Now the fate of Marli's brother is in his hands...and Marli's back in town, stirring up all their old emotions. This time, they'll have to revisit the good *and* the bad to make their second-chance reunion permanent.

#2979 LIGHTNING STRIKES TWICE
Hatchet Lake • by Elizabeth Hrib
Newly single Kate Cardiff is in town to care for her sick father and his ailing ranch. The only problem? Annoying—and annoyingly sexy—ranch hand Nathan Prescott. Nathan will use every tool at his disposal to win over love-shy Kate. Starting with his knee-weakening kisses...

#2980 THE TROUBLE WITH EXES
The Navarros • by Sera Taíno
Dr. Nati Navarro's lucrative grant request is under review—by none other than her ex Leo Espinoza. But Leo is less interested in holding a grudge and much more interested in exploring their still-sizzling connection. Can Nati's lifelong dream include a career *and* romance this time around?

#2981 A CHARMING SINGLE DAD
Charming, Texas • by Heatherly Bell
How dare Rafe Reyes marry someone else! Jordan Del Toro knows she should let bygones be bygones. But when a wedding brings her face-to-face with her now-divorced ex—and his precious little girl—Jordan must decide if she wants revenge... or a new beginning with her old flame.

#2982 STARTING OVER AT TREVINO RANCH
Peach Leaf, Texas • by Amy Woods
Gina Heron wants to find a safe refuge in her small Texas hometown—*not* in Alex Trevino's strong arms. But reuniting with the boy she left behind is more powerful and exhilarating than a mustang stampede. The fiery-hot chemistry is still there. But can she prove she's no longer the cut-and-run type?

YOU CAN FIND MORE INFORMATION ON UPCOMING HARLEQUIN TITLES, FREE EXCERPTS AND MORE AT HARLEQUIN.COM.

HSECNM0323

HARLEQUIN
PLUS

Try the best multimedia subscription service for romance readers like you!

Read, Watch and Play.

Experience the easiest way to get the romance content you crave.

Start your **FREE TRIAL** at
www.harlequinplus.com/freetrial.